AF603991

The Second Fastest Way to Happiness

A Contemporary Romance

By Valentina Ucrós-Acevedo

Hampstead Heath Books

The characters and events in this book are fictitious. Any similarity to real persons, living or dead, is coincidental and not intended by the authors.

Hampstead Heath Books
Bogota, Colombia
Visit our website at www.HampsteadHeathBooks.com

Printed in Colombia

First Hampstead Heath Books edition, October 2022.
Editor and proofreader: Diana Lorena Garcia
Cover images by Kutlay Uyar and Valeriia Miller at:
https://www.pexels.com/@kutlay-uyar-153699421/
https://www.pexels.com/@valeriiamiller/

The Second Fastest Way to Happiness

A Contemporary Romance

1

Hashish

Samuel

11:57 pm – December 2019

The moon hung over the mountains, and an old beggar woman sitting on a snow-covered porch gave me a wicked smile. The kind of wicked smile that you can trust.

The bus was late. I was looking at the moon when a girl came and stood beside me. Her nose was red from the cold, a wool hat covered her face down to her eyebrows, and a thick scarf covered her mouth.

I reached into my pocket, pulled out my Marlboros, took one, and offered her the pack. She looked up at me, all huge brown eyes, and pulled a cigarette out. I lit it for her.

She didn't say thank you and stared across the street, so we both stayed there smoking and freezing. I started to imagine what she would look like naked: tiny breasts, narrow hips, dark nipples. Pretty girls with big brown eyes tend to look alike naked, too.

She moved only to bring the cigarette to her lips. It was past midnight. She spoke, and her voice was lower than I expected.

"Excuse me," the hairs on my nape tingled.

"Yes?" I replied.

"Could I have another cigarette?" The corners of her lips curled up. I noticed a slight accent.

"Sure," I said after a couple of seconds and pulled out the crumpled-up pack of Marlboro Lights. She took the lighter.

"Do you know if bus number 11 stops here?" She mumbled, cigarette hanging from her lips.

"Yeah," I heard myself say. "I don't know why it's taking so long."

A couple of seconds lingered. The cigarette burned and the smoke dissolved into the fog.

"I don't think it's coming," she said.

"No. I don't think so either."

She sighed and narrowed her eyes. The streets were deserted.

It had been a long time since I had slept with a girl. Sophie had been the last one. I left her one week after my father's funeral.

I inhaled sharply.

The girl didn't say anything but kept smoking in the same position, watching me out of the corner of her eye.

"What's your name?" I asked to distract myself.

"Filípa." She answered. "Yours?"

"Samuel."

A car drove past us, its tires squeaking as it turned the corner. We stayed quiet until we could no longer hear the engine.

"Samuel," she said. "That's a nice name."

"Filípa," I replied, letting each letter roll off my tongue. "That's a nice name too."

She took a long drag from her cigarette.

"I can get a taxi and give you a ride if you want," I said, fishing my phone out of my pocket. "It's an app. You can do it yourself if you prefer."

She smiled wider and flung the butt of her cigarette into a pile of blackened snow. It sizzled.

"Samuel," she said, turning to face me, staring into my eyes. The wind blew harder, and her scarf flew behind her back.

"I think I'll walk. I don't live far," she paused and then went on. "You could walk with me if you like."

I rubbed my stiff fingers.

"Which way do you live?" I asked.

She pointed to the northwest of the city.

"It's a twenty-minute walk," she said and then turned to me with a devilish smile. "What do you say?"

I couldn't help but laugh.

"Yeah. Sure. Let's go."

We started walking. The air reverberated with our footsteps, and neither one of us spoke.

Seventeen minutes later, Filípa stopped beside the heavy iron gate of a pre-war building.

"We're here."

The garbage bags in the bins glistened in the rain and the moonlight. A cat screeched.

She fidgeted with her keys.

"Do you—" She started. I noticed that her accent was thicker this time around. "Do you smoke? I—"

She pointed towards the gate with her right thumb, the same hand in which she was holding the keys.

"Yeah," I cut in.

"—have a little hash upstairs." She finished.

We laughed. She turned around and opened the lock.

Her apartment was on the top floor. She climbed the stairs ahead of me, fast. By the second flight, I was out of breath.

She turned several locks to open the apartment's front door and pushed it open with her body. It was warm inside. I took off my coat and scarf and put them on the dining room table. Her jacket lay beside her on the couch, as did her hat and scarf. Her hair was cut short, and it was dark-brown, almost black.

She unzipped her boots and shoved them aside, opened a drawer in the coffee table, and took out an iPod, a speaker, tobacco, a square of hash, and rolling papers.

The apartment's roof was slanted, making a 45° angle with the kitchen counter. There were dishes in the sink. Bread crumbs on the table. A window, big and shut.

She rolled a joint, lit it, and took a long drag. I looked at her. The smoke stayed like a foggy blanket a few centimeters above the table. She brought it to her lips, inhaled one more time, and stretched her arm towards me. I brushed her fingers as I took the joint. The objects in the room had become observers, clouded by smoke they watched, godlike in their indifference.

Filípa was only a few centimeters away, yet the space between us was dense, impenetrable, a bifurcating road across a jungle, a desert, a tundra, an ocean.

She brushed the back of her hand against my stubble, the smoke turned into warm cement, and her lips locked into mine, voracious and demanding as if she too had suddenly felt solid ground beneath her feet. I pressed her body against mine, and she sighed, limp.

"Wait," she breathed.

"Yes?" I asked.

"I don't want to have sex. I want to touch you, and I want you to touch me, but I don't want to have sex. Are you okay with that?"

The seriousness she asked prompted me to look at her more carefully. She came into focus.

"Yeah," I replied. "I'm okay with that."

We fell asleep hours later, huddled together on the tiny living room couch.

9:30am

I woke up early the following day. Filípa was still asleep, her head rested on my arm. I lifted her head with my other hand, careful not to wake her, and stood up. She looked fragile in the morning light. One of her arms was tossed behind her head while the other rested on her stomach. She furrowed her brow and curled into a fetal position mumbling something unintelligible. I walked to the dining table where some of my stuff was laid and was all but ready to leave when I noticed the open notepad. The pages were filled with ballpoint pen and pencil drawings from top to bottom. The traces had been laid down with a fury that compelled me to keep looking. The illustrations were all similar. She drew mostly thin girls with big eyes, sometimes adding wings or pointed ears. I looked back at her; she was still sleeping, her face turned towards the wall. The drawing on the last page was the only landscape. A watercolor painting of the full moon hanging over a violent purple sky. The murderous ballpoint pen traces had been replaced by careful strokes. The colors were clean.

When I looked up, Filípa was staring at me, propped up on her elbows. She cocked her head.

We both listened to the quiet shush of the cars below for a couple of seconds. The apartment was flooded in the pale sunlight.

"Do you want to get breakfast?" She asked.

"Sure," I replied.

Again, we didn't speak while we were walking. Filipa's silence wasn't apprehensive; she seemed to get absorbed by the city, drinking in everything around her with such concentration that I could almost hear the unspoken thoughts. I followed her into a little cafe with small round tables draped in dark green cloth. It smelled of freshly made coffee and croissants. There were no other customers except for an old bearded man drinking a beer by himself. Filípa walked to the counter and turned her head towards me. I got a cappuccino and a Nutella croissant; she got black coffee and a pistachio-ricotta cream-filled brioche. We sat at one of the tables by the window. A flurry of cold air came in every time somebody opened the door.

Filípa tore off a piece of brioche and dipped it into her coffee, bringing it up and down until it broke off from her fingers and floated in the middle, like a sea creature's corpse. She didn't seem to mind.

"Samuel?"

"Yes?"

"Do you think it is possible to fall in love with someone you don't really know?"

She seemed genuinely curious.

"I think it is the only way you *can* fall in love with someone."

"Do you mean you have never fallen in love with someone you knew well?"

She looked almost alien-like, with her huge unblinking eyes and the short dark hair framing her small face.

"It's hard to love people you know well," I mumbled to myself.

She turned her head and stared out the window.

It would snow later. I could tell.

We walked out of the café, and she stood in front of me, hands buried in her pockets. An almost unperceivable rain was falling.

"So...do you have to be anywhere today?" I asked her.

"No. Not really." She replied. "Do you?"

"No."

It was Sunday. Not that it made a difference to me those days. The rain fell harder on the river, and the sun hid behind a wisp of grey cloud.

"Let's go back for a while."

As hard as I tried, I couldn't remember if it was her or me who suggested going back to her apartment to escape the rain. But that's what we did.

It was a Sunday like the epitome of Sundays: Engulfing, drowsy, and grey.

"Do you want a beer?" She asked. It was early, but it was Sunday. I nodded.

She got up and took two beers out of the fridge, opened them, and offered me one. Her sleeve was rolled up, and I could make out two thin ivory lines that crossed her right wrist horizontally. She sat down on the couch, her left leg crossed under her, facing me. I gestured at her wrist.

"You did it the wrong way."

She examined the scars with loving attention.

"Yeah, I know. Plus, it's hard to actually open the skin. If the knife is blunt, it takes forever."

I shrugged, unsure of what to say.

She was rolling a joint, holding the lighter to the now decimated rock of hash, carefully removing bits and mixing them with the tobacco she had taken out of a cigarette.

"How often do you think about it?" I asked.

She laid back on the puff.

"About what?"

"Death."

She chewed the inside of her cheek.

"Often. But not as much as I used to. You?"

"Lately? A lot."

"You are not gonna kill yourself in my apartment, are you?" She teased.

"I wouldn't kill myself here. I mean, no offense, but I don't know you, and who's to say you wouldn't harvest my body parts and sell them on the black market?"

She smiled at me and said:

"Please don't hang yourself, so I can sell your corneas."

I laughed.

She blew out a puff of creamy white smoke and passed me the joint.

"How about pills?" I went on. "Crush them into a powder, mix them with some peach flavor yogurt, plop down on the couch."

"Peach? Are you kidding me?" She asked, arching her left eyebrow.

"What's wrong with peaches?"

"Nothing. It just seems a little too specific to be entirely a joke."

"If it wasn't a joke, why would I tell you? People who want to kill themselves don't talk about killing themselves."

"Categorically untrue." She said. "Haven't you seen *The Bridge*? That documentary about people who jump off the Golden Gate Bridge? Some people talk about it so much that people stop believing them. You know, like that story with the boy and the wolf? Except you're the boy and the wolf."

The smoke nested in the empty spaces.

"So, that's what you'd do?" I asked. "Would you jump off a bridge?"

"I don't think so," she sighed. "Apparently, the fall doesn't kill you. Hitting the water does. You break every single bone in your body."

"You fear pain but not dying."

"Oh, no, I fear dying too."

"So, what, then?"

"I don't know. I thought about carbon monoxide, but cars no longer work like that. You can't just turn on the engine and go to sleep. They don't do that anymore."

Things were becoming hazier; time was going slower. Every second weighed on my shoulders, on my fingers in an altogether pleasant way. She put her feet up on my legs, and I squeezed her toes.

We spent the rest of the day in bed together, playing like children, in between clouds of hashish.

2

An ordinary kind of wrong

Samuel

10:00 p.m.

Some things seem so solid, and then they crumble without notice. Hours later, sadness took over me after I kissed Filípa goodbye and started walking home.

I could see how she was so easily hurtable. I could see that she was all in, which meant I had a free pass to do whatever I wanted.

"Is it possible to fall in love with someone you don't really know?"

I kept walking through the city in the opposite direction that led to my house.

"*Filípa*," I said to myself and tried to call back the feeling I'd had just hours ago while holding her warm body, but there was nothing. She had faded in my mind already.

Women who are ready to give you everything expect everything back. I didn't want or need one more thing to feel guilty about. And I felt bad for her because she was setting herself up to get used as a rag doll. She was giving herself up to me on a silver plate, and I was already enough of a bastard to know that it is never a good idea to do so.

It was a chilly night. Flimsy snowflakes floated in the surrounding wind. I walked into a seedy little bar I had been to once before to kill a bit of time, sat at the bar, and ordered a vodka tonic. The barman was an old man with skin so thin that I could see his pulsing jugular. It was covered by a patchy grey stubble. He put a glass in front of me.

I drank in silence, feeling the vodka making its way through my insides. I tried to picture Filipa's face in my mind and came up with a hazy blend of features surrounding a big, toothy smile.

I finished my drink and signaled the bartender for a second one.

I didn't want to be an asshole. I didn't want to take things to the point where I would have to be an asshole. All I was doing (would be doing) was hanging out with a girl, and that in itself didn't really make me an asshole, except that, for some reason, it felt too close to using her.

I did remember one thing about her body clearly: the mark on her stomach. I remembered touching it, trying to feel the difference in the flesh, but it felt just like the rest of her to my fingers. A misshapen oval of darker skin low and to the right of her navel, the kind of mark a splash of boiling water would leave.

She was broken. That much was easy to see. I had had enough of broken people for a lifetime. I wanted nothing to do with girls who wanted to love me and whom I knew I would inevitably hurt. I finished my drink, put some money on the counter, and left the bar

I was hungry. I went inside MacDonald's, ordered a couple of big macs, fries, and a coke, and made a little nest for myself inside a booth.

Maybe she had been lying, I thought while I stuffed fries inside the burger. Putting on a show for whatever reason. Some women, usually the smart ones, can do that like it's nothing. My dad used to say that women trade one of your problems for one of theirs. I think my father never did like women very much.

I sat there sipping my coke, and I thought about Sophie, even though it was pretty much the last thing I wanted to do. We had fallen into a loop where she didn't believe a word I said, and I was incapable of telling her the truth. I wasn't my best when I was with her, but I wasn't as bad as she made me out to be because, you see, the worse I was, the more she got to be a martyr, and she loved being a martyr. Maybe that's why she never left. She would make a show of leaving me, and then the second I called her back, there she was, ready to forgive everything. I resented and even hated her a little for being so weak. I think I made it clear how I felt about her on more than one occasion. I wanted her to leave. I needed to push her to the limit where she would have to break up with me, but she never left; I had to get my shit together and get out of the apartment for both of our sakes.

Then my father died. Sophie was the first person to be with me. She let me move back into our apartment, and she took care of me, like a baby. She comforted me, I cried on her lap. She cooked for me, ate with me, made sure I didn't smoke too much weed (often unsuccessfully). We were ok for a while, but then I started to feel uneasy. I somehow sensed that she *wanted* me to be a mess.

She wanted to take care of me; she wanted to be my hero, my savior. It repulsed me, the very idea of her whispering sweet nothing's in my ear and stroking my hair. So, I broke up with her again and moved into the big house that my father had left for me. Sophie hated me, but I was okay with that.

I went outside. The streetlamps were on. It had stopped snowing. I started walking again, taking as many twists and turns as possible through the narrower streets.

One cigarette lasted me about three and a half minutes. I smoked one after the other, lighting the new one with the butt of the last.

The vodka and the food were finally making me sleepy.

I hailed a cab and went home. I wanted to forget her because I had worked hard on making a life for myself where the needs of others didn't need to be considered.

I wanted a simple life with my weed, records, and the occasional very expensive escort.

Filípa

The prostitutes who stood by the bridge were old. How much did a woman like that charge? She couldn't imagine anyone paying much for sex with them, with their dresses that looked like they were already out of fashion in the eighties, the smudged mascara, and red dripping lips with the inevitable cigarette hanging from them. Barelegged, with little coats, Filípa felt an odd mix of disgust and fascination: the dyed hair, veiny hands, and the hardened skin of the heel spilling off the edges of their ill-fitting stilettos.

She had smoked the last of her hash with Samuel. He hadn't texted her in 13 hours which probably meant that he wasn't going to; she had to stay busy to avoid dwelling on the fact that she was being rejected. The problem was a general lack of mind distracting artifacts in her apartment at the moment.

Her router was broken. No internet.

Her options included a pile of dirty clothes and the refrigerator (that could use some serious cleaning). There was an entire library at her disposal, but she found herself unable to get immersed in any of the books for longer than one minute until the fidgety feeling itched so much she had to get up and pace around. She knew she was wasting time. Her body felt like it was full of tiny insects biting their way and crawling inside her flesh. Her palms were sweaty. She went out of the living room and into her bedroom.

She wasn't used to the silence. Where she came from, people talked loudly. Here people spoke in hushed tones. Maybe it was the cold.

Gathering what little focus she could muster, she closed the door behind her and looked around. The room was overflowing with stuff: books, broken plastic toys, rocks, flowers, notebooks, flyers, old newspaper articles, pages of magazines, an old broken phone, a plastic V for Vendetta mask with a long crack right down the middle. She felt choked as if each thing was an extra tooth inside her mouth. There was no space for her in that room. Everything, even the pillows, seemed pointy and sharp. She went back out into the living room.

Her hair was matted, there were ashes on her t-shirt. Why did these things seem so important and potentially catastrophic?

She was uncomfortable: her face was puffy, a pimple laid placid on her nose, on her upper lip an incipient Frida Kahlo mustache, the protruding belly falling in three neat terraces of fat.

Filípa craned her neck back and found herself staring at the most spectacular spider web she had ever seen in her life; so intricate in parts it looked milky, and the spiders that paced on it, their legs as thin as the threads themselves. The big bug haphazardly bounced its way right onto the web and continued to quiver a long time after one of the bigger spiders wrapped it up.

It amazed and worried her that she hadn't noticed the spiders.

The park was about 35 minutes away on foot. It was cold. She had never known cold quite like this. She looked out the window. The streetlights were on. Filípa walked into her bedroom, taking long steps, and emerged in jeans, a sweater, a coat, and a scarf.

The building had a long corridor that led to a spiral staircase. She climbed down the five floors fast, jumping the last two steps on every flight. Once she started moving. The cold faded into the background, turning into white noise.

Filípa moved her hips as she walked, serpentine. Little pockets of heat emerged from clusters of people walking down the street. The chalky cloud of her breath almost obstructed her view. Once her body was warm enough from walking, by the time she had crossed the second bridge and passed the Chinese restaurant with the big smiling cat at the front door, her step relaxed. The buildings looked like gentle giants.

She was near the city's center, with its cobbled streets where cars couldn't go and the ancient buildings with stone angels on the rooftops: a capsule of beauty amongst the decadence. A few hundred meters ahead of a giant pigeon-shit-stained statue of some forgotten immortal, a pink neon sign read: *Tout va: Gentlemen's Club.* She stopped by the door.

In her mind, girls in shiny corsets, feather boas, and five-inch heels walked around with murderously sexy stares while men in suits with wallets fat with bills watched. She wasn't sure how much ground *'gentleman's club'* covered. She wondered... her heart thumped in her chest as she imagined herself as one of those girls.

The door opened, she snapped back to reality. A man and a woman came out of the club, both wearing the collars of their coats up so that she couldn't make out their faces. She jumped back and resumed her walking, eyes on the ground. About ten minutes later, she made it to the park.

The wind seeped through the layers of clothing as if trying to touch base with her skin. She locked eyes with one of the figures who leaned against the brick wall on the far end of the basketball court, and he gave her a stare and a nod.

Once with the hash in her pocket, she walked more easily. Her feet wandered without tension through boulevards and alleys, stepping softly on the sidewalks. Filípa was lost in her thoughts; her feet knew the way through this gray and run-down neighborhood, with iron bars over the first-floor windows and dogs that growled as she walked by. A gust of wind sent a plastic cup rattling up the street. Leafless trees stared down at her. She closed her eyes and felt her body respond to the coldness, hairs rising up, cells standing to attention. It was as if, with each inhalation, her body awakened from the inside out. There was an intersection about ten meters ahead. The moon was waxing.

She thought about Samuel standing at the bus stop with his shoulders hunched and his stomach concave in that way only boys can stand and makes them look blasé and vulnerable at the same time. The engorged moon radiated phosphorescent light, and she felt a force at the pit of her stomach pulling her toward him. But of course, the whole thing had just been wishful thinking.

She was embarrassed that she felt a little hurt. Why *was* she hurt? Really, it made very little sense. Since she had arrived at Berkensdorf, she had been on a lot of dates, and a lot of those encounters had fizzled out with neither pain nor glory. All of those guys had gently slipped into oblivion without as much as a whisper. But this time, her thoughts kept trying to redirect her towards *him*, and she found it hard to change their course.

But why? Could I really be so idiotic as to convince myself I'm "in love" with him?

Filípa knew better than that. She had *convinced* herself that she had been in love plenty of times before, sometimes getting close to what she imagined people talked about when they talked about love.

Samuel was intriguing. He looked at her like she was from another planet, and she liked that. She enjoyed seeing herself through his eyes. Or maybe she was just bored and lonely, and he was there.

She couldn't blame him for ghosting her. She had ghosted plenty of people herself, and she had rarely regretted it. So maybe this was karma or, perhaps, it was the chance not to burden someone else with undeserved resentment.

Before she knew it, she was back in front of the iron gate.

Inside her apartment, she played music and smoked until she finally fell into a light sleep, with the headphones still on.

3

Dishes and ghosts

Samuel

It was time to clean the house. In the bathroom, the dirt was spongy. It amassed itself into nausea-inducing dead skin, hair, and soap clots. In the kitchen, the floor felt sticky under the soles of my feet. There were plates in the sink, remnants of uneaten food floated grossly swollen in a thin layer of opaque water, corpse-like. The table was stained with a variety of colors, the gluey shapes peppered with cigarette ash.

I started with the dishes. I took the sponge and put too much soap on it, but that's the way I liked to do the dishes. I took one plate and pretended it was the only thing that existed in the world; I held it, felt its weight, ran my fingers over the painted ceramic, and scrubbed it like I had all the time in the world to be done with that one dish. I opened the water tap, put the soapy dish under the stream, watched as the sods washed away, and clung to my hands like desperate castaways. The counter was cluttered with stuff. A box of salt, a large bottle of extra-virgin olive oil. Paper towels. A pepper shaker. Various rags, all in a lamentable state.

I forgot about the plate and put it back in the sink with the food corpses; grabbed the olive oil, put it in the pantry. I repeated the operation with the saltbox and pepper shaker. I then went back, chose the least dirty rag, and ran it over the newly empty spaces. I stopped myself from dwelling too much on the fact that the rag was filthy. The hardened yellowed skin of the palms of my feet stuck distractingly to the floor. I went inside my bedroom and put on socks, then thought about it and put on flip-flops instead. I went back to the kitchen and over to the sink, where I picked up the only a-minute-ago clean dish and scrubbed it again. I repeated the operation with each item on the sink until there was nothing.

I could feel the soles of the flip-flops sticking to the kitchen tiles as well. The clock ticked. My phone watched silently from the coffee table. I went inside the big drawer with the cleaning supplies and fished for something to wipe the table with.

I found some beige spray that I assumed was some sort of anti-grease liquid, aimed at the surface of the table and fired at will, shooting twice at the hideously deformed blotches of God knows what. I swiped in circles, pretending I was a bartender in the Old West. After it was clean, I ran my finger over the polished surface.

The underbelly of the table was worse; the dirt there had settled in the corners and became black and gooey. I rubbed the underside of the table with a metal sponge dripping anti-grease liquid. Some of the dirt would not go, no matter how hard I rubbed, so I grabbed a knife, pulled it under, and scrapped. The dirt came off like a scab. I ran the drag dripping anti-grease liquid up and down the legs of the table.

I passed the rag through every surface of the kitchen multiple times. I realized too late that the dirt from the table had been transported via the rag to the counter. I took the paper towels and used those instead.

I gathered the stools and chairs and put them on top of the table. Sweeping had an almost meditational appeal. I destroyed the living quarters of the insects and way-too-tiny-for-the-human-eye things that lived on the floor of people's kitchens. I felt like a landlord, evicting squatters. The cobwebs, I couldn't bring myself to completely destroy. I reduced them. But I never killed the spiders. The kitchen was starting to look like a kitchen again. A clean kitchen always struck me as somewhat of a sacred place. So, naturally, I had to desecrate it.

I didn't have much food in the house, but I managed to find half a bag of white rice, a can of tuna, an onion, and half a pepper. Just to make sure, I did one final sweep of the refrigerator's pitiful insides and stroke gold, a few almost dried up leaves of basil sitting placidly at the bottom of the vegetable drawer.

Making rice in a pot without a rice maker is a tricky art that I am proud to have mastered. I poured two cups of water into my medium-sized pot and turned on the gas. The flames in the burner sparked, blue and yellow. I brought them to a slow burn and placed the pot on top. While the water boiled, I julienned the pepper. The onion I cut in half. One half to put into the rice while it cooked, and the other to simmer with the peppers. The knife made a pleasant sound, squishy and then solid, as it cut through the onion's flesh and landed with an echoless thud on the wooden chopping board. The water was coming close to a boil.

I took one of the newly washed spoons from the cutlery drawer, poured one tablespoon of salt into the steaming water, watched intently as it diluted, and then poured in one tablespoon of olive oil. I turned down the flame. There were only low blue flames now. Slowly, I put in the rice. I splashed some olive oil in a saucepan and threw in the chopped vegetables, and put a lid on top.

I turned off the heat on the rice, fluffed it with a fork, and let it sit. The onions were almost transparent and the peppers soft, their skin glistening like worms on the pan. I moved the onions and peppers around with a spatula, turned the heat down until it was an almost static thin blue ring, and turned back to the chopping block. I selected a few basil leaves, pulled them together in a little clump, then chopped them up real small, feeling the thickness of the leaves under the knife, moving my fingers with the blade. I closed my eyes to smell better. The almost decadent sweetness of the peppers and onions had mixed with the freshness of the basil. The rice steamed pleasantly on the counter.

With the spatula, I pushed the rice into the pan to mix it with the vegetables. I only needed half the rice, as it turned out. I put the bowl on the counter, turned the flame back on, and moved the pan back and forth from the handle until there was an even onion-pepper-basil-rice distribution. I added more olive oil.

I took out a fork and a plate, served the food, filled a glass with water from the tap, placed the fork and a knife on each side of the placemat, and folded a napkin triangularly to put under the cutlery. The tuna remained unused.

I put the plate on the table and looked at my work. The stove was splattered with olive oil, there were grains of uncooked rice on the counter, and the sink was filled again. A job well done.

For the first time now, I noticed the silence. The house seemed to be listening. Noisily, the legs of the chair scratching against the kitchen tiles, I got up one last time and took a nearly empty bottle of tabasco from the fridge, sat back down, and shook it violently over my rice. I mixed it, scooped up a generous forkful, and was about to put it in my mouth when my stomach curdled.

A second later, *she* was gone, but I had *seen* her sitting there, ethereal and almost see-through, but real, staring at me with one raised eyebrow and a playful smile on her face. I got up, went around the granite counter, sat on the stool where her ghost had appeared to make sure she wasn't there, and once I was satisfied that it had just been a minor glitch in the Matrix, I sat back down to eat.

I started eating, and the more I ate, the more I realized how hungry I was.

My mind flashed, and suddenly I realized what it was about Filípa that made her so eerie and so familiar at the same time. She smiled just like my mother used to smile. Teasing but warm, a pixyish smile that seemed to mock you and love you at the same time.

I rolled her name around in my tongue alongside the food, savoring each syllable. FI-LÍ-PA.

The last thing a girl like that needed was me in her life. I had been known to take sweet girls and turn them into heinous bitches. Why were girls always either one or the other? Or was it me? I was torn between what I wanted to do and what it felt like I was supposed to do.

"Women," I said out loud.

"Do you think things would have been easier for you if you were gay?"

Her voice rang very clearly in my head. I pictured her sitting in front of me, exactly as I had seen her sitting in front of me at the café the morning that she asked me if I thought it was possible to fall in love with someone I didn't know.

"No," I answered.

Women could make you feel superhuman if they wanted to, but they were capricious in how they dispersed this gift.

I wanted her to be special so that I could feel special. A lover was the second-fastest way towards bliss. The fastest way was weed.

I had moved back into my father's house for one reason and one reason only: more space for my babies. I had a little operation back in my apartment downtown, but here in the big house, I had an entire room with the perfect exposure to sunlight and plenty of water at my disposal. I hardly sold any of what I grew, and mostly my large, very high-quality crops were for my personal use. What I did sell, I sold for a very, very hefty price.

I was afraid to be ordinary, but weed made me feel okay about it. It made me feel special in my normalness.

My days seemed to be headed nowhere. I was terrified I would be consumed by boredom. Killed by the uneventful. Nothing that would fill the pages of novels, nothing but the slow smothering of an otherworldly fire by the dull yet steady waters of ordinary life. I dutifully, lovingly rolled and lit a joint.

She laughed a ghostly laugh from her seat on the other side of the counter.

"What are you laughing at?" I asked rather nastily

"Nothing," she shrugged. I could see my 'grandmother's credence through her flesh. *"I don't know. I just felt like laughing. Is that bad?"*

"No…" I felt chastised. "What are you doing here? Are you here? Did I take LSD and forget about it?" I felt stupid even as I said it. Acid did not make you see perfectly clear images of people while everything else remained flat and normal.

She shrugged again.

"Do you do that often? Take drugs and forget about it?"

"It would depend on the drug."

Alistair, my cat, jumped on my lap and purred. I scratched him behind the ears.

"I think I can hear your thoughts. That makes sense, considering I'm made of your thoughts. Wouldn't you say?"

"I suppose. What am I thinking now?"

"You are thinking about your father, about how he died. You are wondering for the trillionth time if there was anything you did that made it worse or anything you could have done to prevent it. But you already know the answer to that. You know the answer to both of those questions."

I continued to pet my cat.

"You are a particularly unpleasant ghost; do you know that?"

"What happened to your mom? Where is she now?"

"I thought you could hear my thoughts."

"You are not thinking about her."

"Okay. After leaving my dad and me, she stayed at her parents' mountain house for almost a year. Then she rented an apartment in Willenhaven, and she would come to visit me in Berkensdorf, or my dad would drop me off there. Two years went by like that until I was ten. Then she met Rodrigo and moved to Rio. I went to their wedding, but my dad wasn't invited. I stayed with her every summer from when I was ten to when I was fifteen, and then I refused to go anymore. I didn't particularly enjoy my time there. She was happy, yes, and I could see that I *should* be happy for her, but I was bitter too. I hated Rodrigo, I hated his stupid children, I hated the heat. I hated everything."

"They tried to convince you to stay in Rio."

"Yes, but I wanted to stay in Berkensdorf. All my friends were here, and everything I knew. Plus, my dad wasn't bad; he was just not a particularly talkative guy. He worked a lot. Most of the time he spent at home, he was locked in his studio, reading and listening to the radio. I even saw him doing some stretching exercises once. I was alone a lot, and I went out with my friends. They were my family. When I thought about them, I didn't want to leave. As I said, I wasn't particularly fond of Rio."

"Where are your friends now? You strike me as a rather lonely guy."

"Is real Filípa this much of a bitch?"

"I think you know the answer to that, too."

"I haven't talked to them in a while. My friends, that is. I think I just needed some time to be alone."

I felt a pang of pain. I didn't like thinking about my friends. They had tried to be there for me, but I had simply stopped picking up my phone.

I closed my eyes and imagined her naked. When I opened them, she was still clothed.

"Looks like your mind is playing against you. Or maybe you don't actually *want* to imagine me naked. You know, I've always thought that men don't actually think about sex as much as we are told they think about sex. Do they? Do you? It doesn't seem possible."

I squeezed my eyes. I was tired.

"I texted you, you know," ghost Filípa went on.

"I know."

"I thought you liked me."

"I do."

"Then why did you ignore me?"

"*Because* I like you."

She cocked her head and raised an eyebrow.

I got up and went to my bedroom, opened the top drawer on my nightstand, and took out some of my best weed, Green Poison 30% THC. I rolled a fat joint mixed with tobacco and took it back in the living room where I lit it and put on one of my favorite records: BB King's 1969 *Completely well*, which started with my favorite, *The Thrill is Gone.*

I visualized a woman on the couch wearing a velvet dress and long hair, done in a kind of vintage style with curls at the bottom and pinned on the top. She was not Filípa, but she reminded me of her; I tried to make her talk like I had done so successfully in the kitchen, but instead, her eyes shone and her features melted and rearranged, her nose became more aquiline, her eyes more feline, long nails like claws moved to the electric guitar while her shoulders marked the beat of the drums. Her hair changed colors, from very dark it went to almost blonde, and

Sophie was staring at me with her big blue eyes. But it only lasted for a second, and then her hair was short, and she was Lena, that bartender from Trieste, whose face reminded me of a small carnivorous mammal. I willed the vision back into my power and the woman sitting in front of me became Filípa again, her face glowing, her shoulders cutting pale shadows against the dark.

"What would you do if I answered your message right now?" I asked her. "What if I decided to change my mind and nonchalantly reply after three days of silence? Or should I apologize and acknowledge that I was ghosting you? What would that say about me? About you?"

Ghost Filípa smiled and narrowed her eyes.

"How am I supposed to know, Sammy? I am only a very vivid figment of your imagination."

I took my busted smartphone and carefully, very carefully, began crafting a text. The magic might have been lost, I might have already ruined everything, but maybe, just maybe, it wasn't yet too late.

4

The world in technicolor

Filípa

Filípa looked at her phone and hated herself. Here she was, rolling herself down like a red carpet for the next depressed semi-attractive asshole that gave her a little bit of attention. She hated it. She hated herself so much sometimes it was unbelievable. She didn't want to keep begging for decent treatment. She had enough of that with Wallace. One man jerking her around was more than enough. She stopped her fingers before they could finish the reply she had started to write but didn't delete the message. Samuel could fucking wait. He had made her wait long enough.

She then looked at the *other* text she had already sent, and a new wave of self-loathing came over her. It was cringey, needy, sheepish. It was basically an apology mixed with an offer. It was, in a word, desperate.

Why was everything so difficult? She sat back up on the bed, grabbed the miracle of modern technology that was her run-of-the-mill smartphone, unlocked it, and opened the chat with Wallace, the two blue checkmarks beside her message glaring. She decided to call. He was old. He didn't have the same aversion to phone calls that so badly afflicted her generation. She knew he was in town; she knew he was alone, and she knew he was expecting her to contact him. That's the way it always was with him.

What kind of woman did this to herself? *Why?*

She knew what she was doing: Attaching her self-worth to the opinion and approval of the nearest penis-haver. She knew it but knowing it was different from *knowing it,* and when she went on one of the avenues directed by her insecure thoughts, it was remarkably hard to remember that she didn't need anyone to approve of her anymore. She was who she was.

Breathe.

Wallace didn't pick up the phone, and she suppressed the urge to call again or text before it grew bigger. It was hard not to embrace the awful yet familiar feeling of *knowing under any circumstances whatsoever what people thought about her at all times.*

The loop went something like this:

1) Filípa felt that person X was angry, annoyed, or sad.

2) Filípa assumed it was because of something she had said, done, or thought and she proceeded to harass person X to find out what exactly was bothering and how to fix it
3) Person X got annoyed by Filipa's harassment.
4) Filipa's anxiety grew now that *she knew for sure* that person X was angry, annoyed, or sad.
5) Filípa Proceeded to harass person X to find out how to fix it.

Filípa breathed with her whole body and let out a loud sigh with each exhalation. Little by little, the tiny invisible bugs that crawled on her skin and drove her mad started to disappear. Each breath brought a bit of relief. And then, just when she was beginning to relax her neck muscles and ease her thighs, the phone rang, and her stomach tensed automatically.

It was *him.*

"Hello, gorgeous."

She cringed. Filípa hated being called out on her appearance, even if it was a compliment.

"Wallace, you know I don't like that."

The phone was slippery with sweat. Wallace laughed.

"Learn how to take a compliment, kid."

Normally Filípa would have replied something cheeky, but she wasn't in the mood. She felt deflated and angry, though she couldn't quite tell at what or whom.

"I texted you," she said. "You left me on read."

Wallace scoffed.

"Don't give me that Filípa, you know I don't follow your silly millennial WhatsApp ethics code."

Now she was getting really angry. It was difficult, but she swallowed it.

"How long are you staying in town?" She asked instead.

"Just a couple of days. Then I'm off to Rome, and then Oslo for a conference. Then if everything goes according to plan, I'll come back to Berkensdorf for a couple of weeks for some quiet time. I've rented a house by the lake, and I've half a mind to take you with me. What do you say?"

Filípa bit her lip.

"Can I see you tonight?" She asked.

"Not tonight. But after I come back, I promise. Oh, and, Filípa?"

"Yes?"

"Helmut Hollander is putting together a little something in his gallery, and I might have dropped your name. I think your watercolors might sell well. Perhaps he'll give you a bit of space."

He was always doing this, and she seldom followed through. Filípa loved to paint, she had always loved to paint, but she was sure that in the end, she would find a job somewhere and live off of that while painting in her spare time to soothe her soul. Wallace's casual dismissal of the need for money astounded her. It was a characteristic of the rich, of course. It never ceased to amaze her just how blasé they could be about something that so thoroughly dominated other people's lives.

Filípa wasn't poor, but she was on a budget. She came from a middle-class family; her parents were hard-working people who, through massive effort, had managed to send her to the northern hemisphere to study in a fine arts academy, pretty much the most useless thing that anyone could choose to study. Filípa had wondered many times why her parents had such blind faith in her. It scared her. She felt like a thief because the truth was, she had little or no confidence in herself.

In her mind, anyone paying her a compliment, anyone being nice to her was lying. They wanted something. To hurt her, to mock her, to use her.

Whenever Wallace mentioned one of his art-world friends who could potentially help her, she balked. *It's my curse*, she told herself.

On the other end of the phone, Wallace cleared his throat.

"Filípa? Are you there?"

She took a deep breath and concentrated on the cool air at the tip of her nose.

"Hollander? Is that the little one with the bow tie?"

"No, that's Marquez. Hollander is the one who wears the flower ties with the red leather loafers."

"Right! Okay. I'll do it—What do I have to do?"

He laughed a hearty belly laugh. The sound of it always made her smile.

"Go to his office and leave your portfolio with Andrea. Leave a contact number as well, and if you are selected for the show, they'll get in touch with you. And don't do that thing you do where you don't pick up the phone and then pretend you didn't see the missed call."

"I don't do that—"

"Yes, you do. I know you, don't play games with me. They don't work."

Filípa felt a tingling under her navel. Her voice dropped an octave when she answered. It took on a sultry quality.

"Okay— I promise."

"Good. Start working on your portfolio. Make sure you include those elegant nudes you showed me the other day, the ones drawn over the bone paper with black ink."

"Okay."

"I'll call you. Bye."

He hung up. He was always like that. Giving her orders, organizing her life. She knew he did it out of kindness; but it still left her with a bitter taste in her mouth. It felt a little like accepting charity. She shook off the thought. It was her curse. The pride of the wounded. She tried to relax once more. Why was relaxing so difficult?

Her portfolio was done. Her watercolors were carefully placed inside plastic pockets, all bound up inside a binder. She had nothing else to do to the portfolio but add a couple of the newest pieces, the elegant, continuous lines forming lanky male and female bodies, resting, unassuming… *relaxed.*

She felt like something was missing. She was angry at Wallace. She wanted to tell him to stop giving her instructions, even if he meant well. She wanted to tell him that it was rude of him to assume she was always available for him, even if she was. She wanted to kick him in his stupid face and yell at him that she knew how much pleasure it gave him to control her, to keep her on edge. She knew he enjoyed the power imbalance of their relationship. Her anger was there, but it wouldn't take full form; she wouldn't allow it.

She felt the need to *do* something. Back on the table laid her sketchbook. She glanced at it, and the memory of Samuel looking through it bubbled to the surface.

She opened the fridge. Behind a jar of olives and an empty ketchup bottle was a shiny tin can with a plastic lid. She took it out and opened it. Wrapped under many, many layers of saran wrap was a single tiny square of bright paper. With slippery fingers, she cut the square into two triangles. One of those, she put on the tip of her tongue and sucked it like candy. The feeling was familiar, and yet it always caught her by surprise.

Once it hit, she started moving her body, the delicious fire coursing through her veins and putting the world in technicolor.

Acid felt good.

She conjured Samuel's image and yelled at it:

"How come you ignored me for three days, you miserable piece of shit? Is this your M.O.? Are you the kind of guy who believes that bullshit about how being mean to women makes them love you? Newsflash, asshole: it only makes us hate ourselves. Big surprise! A depressed girl will go for people who mistreat her. Men are fucking brilliant. Just *brilliant*."

She took on the 'role' of Samuel now. She imagined him remorseful and begging. She pictured herself towering above him and kicking his midsection hard. He moaned.

"I swear it's not you, Filípa. It's me."

Filípa laughed out loud, putting as much scorn as she possibly could into her voice.

"That's your excuse? That's what you're gonna tell me? The most typical, tired, lazy, stupid cliche of all time? *It's not you; it's me.* Fucking seriously?"

She was so angry she punched the air. Fury amassed itself like a ball of energy inside of her, and she *wanted to hurt him.* Not just emotionally. She felt like a Countess of old, plotting to poison her horrid husband to finally be able to enjoy his fortune in peace. At that moment, she felt completely justified in her actions. In her mind, she fed Samuel arsenic and watched him writhe in pain. *You deserve this,* she told Ghost Samuel. *You made me do this to you.* Ghost Samuel vomited and shat himself, and all the while, she danced around him as he implored her forgiveness, pleaded for mercy, and she just watched, like a Goddess, as his life left his body. *You deserve this,* she told his wretched corpse. *This is all your fault.* His head twisted, and a macabre smile was painted on his blue lips.

The dead mouth twisted, and out came a croak, a sound that clawed at her stomach like Prometheus' eagle.

Stupid men, she thought. *Stupid, stupid, stupid.* Always thinking that they had the upper hand. Always assuming that their way of seeing the world was the correct one. She envied them; she envied men and their blind faith in themselves. She felt full of doubt. How did they do that? Walk around the globe with the absolute certainty that they were the embodiment of everything right? Of everything as it should be? And more than that, how did they manage to convince women that *they,* the men, were the measuring stick for which everything else was to be held? What made them think their way was the only way? How could they believe that there was only one way to do anything at all? Filípa turned her head to the corpse of Samuel's ghost, which was strangely enough not a corpse anymore, but a specter, a translucent reproduction of the real person who was, in that very moment, sitting in his living room, doing whatever it was that people do when they aren't being watched.

"What do you think, Sam? Why are men the masters of the universe when they are so thick in the head?"

Ghost Sam laughed.

"It's all about faith, babycakes. What do you believe in, little girl? Do you still believe a knight in shiny armor is coming to save you?" He laughed again, without bitterness. He was genuinely having fun.

"No," Filípa replied, her cheeks red. "I know that there is no knight in shining armor. I know I'm supposed to save myself." Samuel looked into her eyes, a question there. She avoided it. "I don't want you to save me, she told him. That's not what I want."

"What do you want, Filípa? Tell me. Anything at all."

Filípa looked at her hands. She wanted to say that she didn't know what she wanted, but that wasn't quite true. She knew what she wanted, but it was a feeling that refused to be put into words. It was there, though. And she wanted *it.* She wanted *it* so bad.

Filípa flapped her arms around like wings, she danced until her body felt tired. Not too tired, the acid would prevent that. She flailed her arms and kicked her legs, and occupied as much space as she wanted to. Her small body wasn't small at all. It was huge, a universe. It was *all,* she thought as she touched it, and it was so funny that it was so solid, so real, and yet most of the time, she wasn't really aware that it was there. Ghost Samuel had vanished. Everything seemed new now, like she was seeing it through different eyes. All of her furniture, all of her things that were only an extension of herself into the world. Another hand, another mouth, another nose, another toe. How greedy, and yet how natural it all seemed.

5

The gallery

Filípa

On the night of the exhibition, everything started wrong. The dress she had wanted to wear had a huge stain on it, and she had spent 45 extra minutes frantically looking for another suitable outfit until she finally just said "fuck it" and put on jeans. She slapped on some makeup carelessly, and the results showed it; her face seemed ugly to her as she glanced at it for the last time in the mirror. But time was running out. She was already very late.

One thing she had come to notice was that it was important to build the right walls around yourself. It wasn't isolation; it was protection. Filípa had gone from living behind a dark, tall wall with a shadow so impenetrable she couldn't even see herself, to having no walls at all and being completely open, to where she was now: somewhere in between.

The right walls allow you to stay sane when you encounter something antagonistic. It is naive to think every interaction you have will be a pleasant one. Therefore, you must learn how to react when being attacked in a way that gives you a chance to win. If you get angry, if you resort to emotional appeal to get your way, you have already lost. Crying and yelling may work with your mother, but it will hardly work on anybody else. But the question is, how not to react personally and take it personally when someone does something that hurts you? The right kind of walls help. They are not tall walls, and they are see-through. If you can keep the attacks behind the wall and detach yourself from the situation, then you might be able to deal with it without it getting dirty.

Filípa sighed and waved away a waiter offering her a flute of champagne. Mentally she repeated over and over the Litany Against Fear from Dune.

"I must not fear.
Fear is the mind-killer.
Fear is the little-death that brings total obliteration.
I will face my fear.
I will permit it to pass over me and through me,
and when it has gone past,
I will turn the inner eye to see its path.
Where the fear has gone, there will be nothing.
Only I will remain."

She had been doing this lately after reading Chapter House for the second time. She tapped her index and her thumb inside her pocket.

Wallace was ignoring her, of course, and it didn't look like anyone was interested in her paintings. She felt rather out of place, looming around her framed watercolors in case anybody wanted to talk to her, which nobody did. She'd already had a couple of glasses of champagne and was starting to feel light-headed.

"Better stop now," she thought as she reached for another flute from a tray. That ugly little voice was starting to creep up on her as she watched Wallace talking to an older blonde woman, that little worm of a thought that told her that he had no right to treat her like that, that he was a miserable cockroach, that she would not let him get away with treating her like that. A strong desire to throw a glass of champagne, not its contents, a *glass* of champagne at his face overcame her.

People around her were all in little clusters, talking to each other, laughing. A man bumped into her on his way to say hello to someone else. A young woman in her twenties approached one of the paintings. The one with the naked man and the cat. She stared at it for a couple of seconds, and when Filípa was working up the courage to introduce herself, she smiled politely and moved on.

This was miserable. Self-promotion was not what people thought about when they decided to become artists, but it was a big part of the job.

She grabbed another glass of champagne. The more she drank, the louder the voice got and the harder it was to concentrate on the Litany. She wanted to right the wrong that was being done to her, walk over to Wallace, and at least force him to say hi, from student to teacher. Nobody said that he had to kiss her in the mouth, for Christ's sake!

Why did he have such a massive ego? Why did he deny her the tiniest drop of respect and trust that she would not cross the boundaries? He treated her like a child or like a dog. Or even worse, he was stupid enough to think that if he didn't treat her like shit from time to time, she would fall hopelessly in love with him. She knew what they were. What they were not. She wasn't stupid, and she hated being treated as such.

Normally she would have been able to talk herself out of it by reminding herself that the only thing she had control over was her own actions and that if she lost control and demanded him to acknowledge her, she would only be proving him right in his perception.

Alcohol made her feel warm and fuzzy. She drank the rest of her champagne and took another glass. She was feeling bold, sexy, and most of all, stupid.

"I mean, who the FUCK does he think he is anyway?" She muttered under her breath.

First, he practically MADE her submit the watercolors. Then, when she got selected, not a word. No congratulations, no well done: just silence. Then she got the absolute worst corner in the gallery, and when she got here, they told her they only had space for three of her paintings, not five, as it had been originally stated. Finally, there were the side looks and the cold manner in which the employees and the owner had treated her.

She was starting to suspect Wallace had not been quite as tight-lipped about their relationship as he had led her to believe.

Art, of course, is subjective. She knew she had talent. She knew she painted from the heart and that she minded her technique. But she also knew that if somebody pointed at her and labeled her 'the student who was fucking her teacher', that would immediately taint her paintings as less worthy, less valuable: her value as an artist was immediately diminished, and that hurt because it wasn't her painting's fault that she was dumb enough to think that an older, married man who also happened to be an important professor would not brag about fucking a stupid little 26-year-old from his class. She was sad for them, for the watercolors. It wasn't their fault they were attached to her.

She had lost count of how many glasses of champagne she had drunk. Walking around the gallery, she had to hold on to a stranger's shoulder to keep her balance. The guy turned from his conversation, annoyed, but she ignored him and kept walking towards Wallace in what she hoped was a straight line.

"I need to talk to you."

"Excuse me," he said apologetically to the ugly, bird-like woman in the hideous green dress that he was talking to. "Miss Alvarez, hello." He grabbed her by the elbow and pushed her towards a corner

"Let go of me!" She muttered angrily as she tore her arm from his grip, but he held on tighter.

"You're drunk. How much did you have? I saw you down at least four glasses—"

"Oh, so you fucking *noticed* I was here." She snapped, and a couple of people turned their heads towards them. Wallace angrily grabbed her arm and basically pushed her towards the exit. She tried to walk faster because he was practically dragging her, and the alcohol bouncing in her stomach was making her nauseated.

"Stop—stop, I said *stop*!" They were out in the street, but he didn't let go of her arm, instead, he pulled her closer to him, menacing, huge. His face was carved in stone, and his lips barely moved when he spoke.

"I will not tolerate any more of these little outbursts, do you understand me? I work with these people. I had to call in favors to get you into the show, and this is how you repay me?"

Filípa started feeling hot, humiliating tears welling up in her eyes.

"I didn't ask you to do that," she spat, jerking her arm, trying to free it, but he wouldn't let go.

"You're drunk. Go home and sleep it off. I'm going back inside now. Do *not* follow me."

"Pedazo de MIERDA. I want *nothing* from you." Filípa screamed, not giving half a rat's ass who heard her.

Wallace, certainly, pretended that he hadn't.

6

Everybody pays

Samuel

The last voice call I received was from my aunt when my father died, so, naturally, when my phone rang at 3:23 in the morning, I nearly had a heart attack. Too stunned to even be annoyed that someone dared call at this ungodly hour, I picked up.

"Hello?" My voice was thick with sleep.

"Hey," Filípa sounded wide awake, agitated. I could hear street sounds. "Listen, can I come over to your house? Like, now?"

I sat up in bed in a heartbeat.

"Sure. I'll text you the address."

"Great." She hung up the phone.

An hour and fifteen minutes later, the doorbell rang. Had she walked? She was wearing the same wool hat, scarf, and jacket as the other night. As soon as I opened the door, she lifted a blue plastic bag. The contents clinked.

"I brought beer."

I took the plastic bag from her and stepped back to let her in. We went into the kitchen, opened the beers, and she leaned on the marble counter. Her eyes kept bouncing off of every wall like she wasn't really sure what to do with herself. I took a step towards her, and she flinched.

"Sorry," I said, a little confused.

She looked up at me. Her cheeks were flushed. She shook her head.

"I—I'm sorry. I don't know why," she whispered, making an effort to keep her voice steady, only half-succeeding. Something about her demeanor moved me.

I pulled her to me, engulfing her small frame entirely. She leaned into me easily, buried her nose in my chest, and she hugged me back. I closed my eyes and tried hard to stop thinking because, if I did, I would break the fragile equilibrium that had somehow arisen between us, a kind of intimacy that could so easily become weird. It only takes one wrong move; the weight shifts, and you can't look into each other's eyes. Once you start thinking a fight or flight response is activated, and you either make it all into a joke, or you let it rot. Either way, the easiness is gone. And that's terrible.

I said nothing. I just held her, closed my eyes, and tried to focus all of my attention on each breath. The tension slowly left her body. I kissed her forehead, and we untangled at the same time. She looked different now. More at home. Her cheeks were still flushed, and her lashes were wet, but she was kind of smiling, and her eyes were no longer bouncing all over the place.

"Smoke?" I asked.

She nodded and followed me into the living room. Once there, she sat on the big Ottoman chair while I stretched my legs on the leather couch and smoked weed from my water pipe. She dug through her backpack, looking for something. It was a small spiral notebook, the kind that children use for school. She opened it and started sketching with a blue fountain pen.

I stared at her shamelessly, at the dip between her clavicles and the swell of the breasts under her t-shirt. What was intriguing was that she seemed at ease with being stared at. If she could tell I was watching her, she didn't seem to mind. If anything, I'd say she liked it.

She became completely absorbed in her drawing. I got up to put on music. My most precious possession, and probably the only thing I actually gave a damn about in the entire house, was an old turntable and, of course, the collection of records that my father had amassed throughout the years. I chose something I thought she might like. The Velvet Underground & Nico, 1967.

Femme fatale started playing. I noticed how she smiled and nodded approvingly; I felt idiotically pleased.

Filípa shifted and sat up before looking into my eyes. Without talking, she walked over to the couch, wrapped her legs around my waist, and kissed me, her lips lingering before she pulled away.

I tried to kiss her again, and she backed off. Her smile turned into a snarl, and her hand flew into my cheek so hard I felt my teeth vibrate.

I screamed, holding my face in complete disbelief.

"What the fuck?"

"Hit me back." She said.

I took a deep breath.

"I want you to hit me back." She repeated.

I didn't move.

"What's the matter? What are you afraid of?" It was no question. It was a challenge.

The hairs on my nape stood up. I could feel my fingers pulsing.

When she moved to slap me again, I grabbed her by the wrist and pushed her off me. She stared at me from the carpet and got up as I got up from the couch and backed her into the wall. Heart pumping, I punched her in the stomach, just hard enough for her to feel it.

She bent over slightly and moaned.

"Is this what you want?" I whispered, her face just millimeters away from mine.

Her voice came out airy.

"Yes."

I kissed her, and she bit me so hard I tasted blood.

7

The kiss

Filípa

11:39 am

Filípa woke up with her whole body hurting. Her neck was stiff. She sat up. They had somehow made their way up to his grey and blue bedroom. A window to the east let in the rays of light poking through the blinds, a writing desk on the left side corner was home to a MacBook Air and a few scattered pens.

Samuel was knocked out, a thin thread of saliva hanging from his open mouth. She climbed down from the bed, threw on the first thing she found on the floor, a hoodie and his boxers, tiptoed out of the bedroom and down the stairs into the living room.

Filípa rubbed her eyes, ran her fingers through her short dark hair, and looked around the room. Sun poured in through the skylight on the roof. The whole place had the feeling of pancakes in the morning, of things comfortable in an uncomfortable world.

She went back upstairs, gliding her hand on the banister. Samuel's bedroom was to the left; a half-open door caught her attention to the right. She turned towards it and pushed the door open. It turned silently on its hinges.

She was inside a big studio. A massive writing desk dominated the room. There were moldings on the ceiling, and the walls were bare, except for a bookcase filled with heavy volumes with titles like *"Current Diagnosis and treatment in Hepatology"* and *"Endoscopy and Advanced Practice Psychiatric Medicine: Integrating Psychotherapy, Psychopharmacology, and Complementary and Alternative Approaches."*

Doctors. Psychiatrists. She looked away from the books feeling slightly nauseated.

It was only when she turned around that she saw it. Filípa got sucked into paintings as most people get sucked into movies. She followed the line of the man's neck, then stopped for a long second on his hands, which held the woman's face with a sort of furious tenderness. With her gaze' she caressed the fabric of their clothes and touched the woman's pale shoulder, which in her mind felt as cold as marble, despite the aura of yellow light around it. The painter's name and the date of the painting were written in bold black letters at the bottom of the poster, but Filípa didn't need to look at them to know that this was *The Kiss* by Gustav Klimt, completed between 1907 and 1908. Her eyes then focused on the woman's hand, on her bent fingers which dug into his flesh, though her face was turned away from him.

Filípa closed her eyes and felt the specks of light like tepid snowflakes on her face.

Coffee, she thought and made her way down to the kitchen. Carefully, because she had a tendency to break or damage any appliance or electronic device that was unlucky enough to cross her path, she emptied the old coffee into the sink, rinsed the pot, and filled the machine with water until it marked 4 cups, replaced the filter, put four spoons of grounded coffee beans inside and shut the lid. The machine gurgled happily, and soon the scent of freshly made coffee overwhelmed the air.

She took a clean mug from the sink, walked to the coffee maker, and poured herself a cup. In the kitchen, everything looked soft, dust slowly twirled in pools of light, steam emanated from her mug in spirals.

As she took the first sip, it occurred to her that she had always been rather careless with her things. It had never been hard for her to give away what she owned: books, clothes, even money; she had never felt particularly attached to any of it. She gave away her things, lost them, or managed them without care until they broke. It had taken her a while to realize, and it was still hard to grasp sometimes, that most people were the opposite. They took care of their things. They minded themselves.

She was even more careless with her body than she was with her objects and found that she kept forcing herself to do things she didn't want to do. This was most evident when it came to sex. She had slept with a total of 23 men and two women, but if someone would have asked her how many of those people she had actually desired, she wouldn't have known what to say. The thrill she got from sex didn't come so much from the act itself but more from the performance that preceded it. She could almost always tell who they wanted her to be without them even saying a word. A sweet, vulnerable girl. A jaded vixen. A friend. A toy.

I don't know how to be a person in the world. I don't understand the rules.

A noise upstairs pulled her back into reality. Before her mind could register what her body was doing, she put the mug down on the counter and jumped down from the stool. Luckily most of her clothes and her backpack were in the living room. With a sense of urgency, she put on her jeans, buttoned up her shirt, jammed her feet into her shoes without undoing the laces, swung the strap of her bag across her shoulder, and walked out the door without looking back.

After about ten minutes of walking, she passed by a playground. No children were playing. Filípa sat on a swing. The ice in the chains snapped and crackled under her weight. She reached inside her backpack for her tobacco, rummaging through the pile of useless papers, broken notebooks, and articles of clothing until she finally found it; then repeated the operation until she had found the filters and rolling papers as well. She tried rolling a cigarette, but the tobacco kept sticking to her hand, and the paper kept falling apart between her fingers; her palms were sweating that much. She gave up and put her palms up against the wind, so the brown flakes floated away. Her heart was pounding against her chest. She was afraid, though she couldn't quite tell why.

After a while, she got up and started walking. An old woman looked at her from a window, but she didn't notice.

Once inside her apartment, she went directly into the bathroom and turned the water tap all the way to the left. She liked the water scalding hot, and it took a while to get that way. So very slowly, almost ritualistically, she began to undress. The bath was almost full by the time she got to her socks; these were always the last to go. She avoided touching the bathroom floor and skipped directly from the fuzzy blue bath mat and into the water. Water vapor dripped from the little bathroom window at odd intervals, splattering delicately on the window sill, the water making soft gurgle sounds as it tapped against the porcelain walls of the tub. Some of the tiles above the toilet were mirrored, an unsuccessful attempt by the previous resident to bring some sort of artsy vibe into the apartment. Filípa breathed in the vapor and let it settle inside like a cloud of Novocain, eyes shut. Her body was completely limp. She opened her eyes and caught a glimpse of her face in one of the little mirrored tiles.

It still struck her how different she looked without long hair. Hair has memory. It carries. People don't realize how much they carry in their hair.

Filípa put her head under the water and screamed. Nothing of that scream was audible to the world. But it was a war cry.

8

Thirty-year-old men with low self-esteem can't make grown-up decisions

Samuel

"...I don't care. I don't care anymore. Ok. I'll leave. I'll go. There is nothing I can do here anymore. There is nothing I can say to you right now to make things better."

The woman reaches for the man's hand, and he slaps it away, an expression of disgust on his lips. She shuts her eyes and clutches her stomach, doubles over, as if in physical pain.

"Fine. I'm sorry. I'm so sorry. I've ruined everything. Again. Please forgive me, I beg you. This can't be happening, this can't be the end, this isn't real. It can be okay, please—Please, I meant no harm, I swear. We were just out, and it was just one drink. I hadn't drunk in so long. I got drunk faster than usual, okay? You don't believe me. I can tell by your face. Fine. Don't believe me, I can do nothing about it. I was being stupid, as usual. Please, forgive me."

A light breeze comes in through the open window, and the curtains billow. After a while, the silence gets loud, and the woman speaks again.

"I'm not leaving. I'm not. Never. Please. Please. I beg you. Where are you going? Talk to me! please, just talk to me, tell me why you are so angry!"

A couple of minor implosions seem to take place under the man's skin. He is livid.

"No, no, no, that's not what I meant at all, I meant just, wait, listen, listen, now, don't, I will not move, look at me, I didn't mean that you have to explain why you are angry, I get why, I understand it perfectly, and you have every right to be mad, every right in the world, I know that, ok? I fucked up, and I'm here, and I'm begging you to forgive me, and I have no excuses for myself, but if you talk to me, maybe there is something else that is bothering you, maybe you want to tell me something, and you don't know how—"

The woman's arms flap like wings while she talks. Her voice is thick with tears, and her hair is disheveled. The man sits on the edge of the bed, smoldering with anger; a low hum as if from an engine seems to come out of him.

The man on the bed speaks, and his voice is the hard whisper of barely controlled anger.

"I want you to leave."

The woman's arms stop flapping. She is defeated. Arms at the waist, head hung, she moves toward the open suitcase on the bed and closes it. Her husband's head is up, and he is looking towards the door, where Sammy is standing in his footed pajamas, wide-eyed, clutching a toy car close to his little chest. A wave of tenderness washes over the woman, her brow relaxes, and she smiles sweetly at the little boy. She walks toward him, picks him up, and wraps her arms as tight as she can around his little body, trying to get every centimeter, every scent, to create a solid memory of him in her mind.

The little boy looks down.

I woke up drenched in a cold sweat.

My mother and my father. They could not have been more wrong for each other, but they stayed married for fifteen years, which isn't really that much when you think about it. But I don't really understand how they stayed married for even two. My mother, with her dozy mind, her inability to focus on anything for more than thirty seconds, her huge, welcoming heart, her eyes that existed only to tell you that you were beloved, her utter discomfort in bureaucratic buildings, the way she used to squeeze my shoulder and the tightness in my stomach would go away. My beautiful mother, who believed the world was ultimately a good, gentle place, and who failed to see, until the end, how completely wrong her approach was. People were good and kind to *her* because *she* was good and kind, had money, and was pretty. She was heartbroken and confused when someone didn't fit this mold, every time she would feel betrayed and she would crumble, like a child who has been lied to for the very first time.

And my father. My father, with his inability to let go of anything, his mania for controlling the world around him down to the very last detail, his distaste for the mess, his utter contempt for art. Perhaps when they met, they were different people. Perhaps something happened, and by the time I met them, they had changed.

Filipa's bra and panties were on the floor. I listened to the sounds around me for a second and heard nothing except for the cars outside. I took a deep breath, got up, and made my way into the bathroom, where I splashed cold water on my face. A purple bite marked my neck. I traced the mauve edge with my finger.

I picked up her bra from the floor. It was pink lace, with blue daisies painted on the straps. Running my fingers through it, my mind went back to the image of my fingers wrapped around her neck.

Up until that day, I had never hit a woman in any context. Girls are not to be touched, *not even with a flower*. Something my father used to say.

I remember that in all their fights, it was always my mother who did the yelling, crying, begging, and threatening. My father would sit, stone-faced, and say nothing or speak in a very low tone. He would sit there until she got too tired or left. He would be silent for days on end after that. My mother would sit glossy-eyed across from me on the breakfast table, her hair a mess, shoulders slumped, and he would come in, fill his thermos with coffee and walk out, his presence magnified by his silence, every step, every cupboard opened startling us like a firecracker. Her knuckles would get white from squeezing her mug so tight. Then we would hear the front door slam, and the air would get a little less dense. She would smile at me then and say something along the lines of "*Do you want some chocolate milk, Sammy? How about pancakes?*". Those were the best mornings. She would keep me home from school, and we would eat breakfast and then go up to her studio, where she would lay down newspapers on the floor and then let me dip my fingers into her acrylics and play. She sat behind her canvas and popped up from behind, and gave me a smile every now and then. Then, at noon, she would bring up grilled cheese and tomato sandwiches for us to eat on the floor; paint all over our clothes. As the afternoon went on, eventually, we would get tired of painting, and we would cuddle up in her room and watch a movie on VHS. If my father had to work the night shift at the hospital, we would order a pizza and eat it in bed. My mother never cared about the crumbs; my father would always tell her off in the morning. He didn't get angry, though. He lectured her calmly, which even as a five-year-old, I found to be demeaning. And my beautiful mother would become dim and shut down. From a fierce lioness, she shrunk to a frightened alley cat. I could see that as I grew, the lioness moments became fewer and further apart.

By the time she left, when I was eight years old, a part of me understood her. My father insisted on keeping me, and she didn't put up much of a fight. I don't know who I hated more.

People don't give kids enough credit. I noticed everything. I heard every fight. I felt my mother tensing and my father fuming. Kids know.

My father never talked about her. If I did, he would go into silent mode. It was as if she had never existed. He banished her. The canvases, acrylics, the oil paintings, the watercolors, the sketch notebooks; all gone. He got rid of most of the artwork she had bought for the house, but for some reason, he kept a poster in his studio. I watched, and I saved what I could. A charcoal sketch of us in the park she framed for me when I turned seven, a small oil painting of a ballerina sitting on a park bench on a sunny day, and a jeweled box that I would use later in my teenage years to stash my weed.

I made my way down to the kitchen, put two slices of white bread in the toaster, and poured myself a glass of milk.

Filípa had asked me to do things that I realized I had wanted to do for a long time. It felt good to put her completely under my control, make her do what I wanted. Never before had I allowed myself to think that maybe there was a part of me that wanted to hurt a woman. "*But I asked you to,*" Filipa's voice sounded clearly in my head. Who had been in control, really?

It was almost 2:00 pm already. The bread jumped; I grabbed it with my fingers, tore off a piece, dipped it into the milk, and ate it. I didn't have much to do today. I was out of a routine. I made my way into the living room and put the record back in its case. My boxers and my hoodie were slumped on the floor. I left them there. Where was she? Back in the kitchen, I ate the other piece of toast and went over to make coffee, to see that she had made coffee; the pot was sitting full and warm in the machine. The house was silent. She was not there.

On the counter, I noticed a half-full mug. So, she had gotten up, put on my boxers, made coffee, and left. Something told me she had been elsewhere in the house. It was a big house. I made my way around, trying to spot anything that looked out of place, looking for clues of her presence. I found one on the second floor. The door to my mother's old studio, which my father had turned into a second library, was open.

Light poured in. I went behind the desk and sat on the leather chair. Nothing looked real. I was dreaming again. Except usually when I dreamed, I saw myself from the outside. It couldn't be, I decided as I looked at my hands.

There was nothing quite different about the room, yet it felt different somehow. Dust swirled into whirlpools, the afternoon light made hard edges softer, the whole room was a deep, languid kiss.

I sensed that Filípa was the kind of person that responded to the slightest pressure by running away. If I wanted to keep her around a little longer, I would have to let her dictate the terms of endearment.

Girls like Filípa are like cats. You let them come to you.

Days passed, but she didn't re-appear. My mind started playing tricks on me, showing me scenarios where she was dead, mutilated, and it was all my fault because I had let her go.

I was getting better at avoiding going down the paths directed by my thoughts. It was simple, but breathing did work. Thoughts could be very convincing, so it was important not to argue with them.

I had come close to breaking my rule of letting her come to me a couple of times, but I had managed to restrain myself. I searched for her in the faces of strangers in the streets, hoping I would casually run into her at the movies, at an art exhibition, at a bookstore, anywhere… the kind of thing that happens in movies, but not in real life.

She needs me, I kept thinking, and then I kept swatting the thought away as exactly the kind of thing I shouldn't think.

My first impulse was to go to her apartment, but I discarded the idea. Again, it seemed like the kind of thing that would scare away any girl with good reason. I grabbed my phone and tried to decide what to write to her. I typed and deleted five different versions of a text, but somehow everything I wrote looked terrible regardless of how smooth it sounded in my head. I kept going like this, deleting and typing, before I decided that I was unsuited for the task of trying to regain a girl whom I had clearly turned away by trying to give her the cold shoulder when I should have gone after her the second I realized she was gone. *Come back.* I finally typed. *Whenever you want.* Then I deleted it, letter by letter, and put the phone away.

I had the distinct feeling within me that there was something I was forgetting. Something I had not seen, left behind somewhere in the house, and it was there, this unnamed object, begging, calling for me to come to pick it up. I moved with a strange heaviness, my limbs tired and aching as if I had exercised a lot. I went upstairs; the wooden stairs creaked under my weight. These past few days, I'd been spending a lot of time in the studio. The room was strange yet familiar. Being in it was like being in a lukewarm pool. Not quite pleasant, not quite uncomfortable either. It was *there*, surrounding me, the air heavy, the dust alive. Ruling over the space was the big, mahogany desk with the elegant leather chair behind.

My father had been a doctor who specialized in practical psychiatric epidemiology. He was very well regarded in his field, and I remember feeling a deep sense of pride as a child on the rare occasions he took me to the hospital with him. Other times my mom and I would pick him up after a long shift, during a period when we only had one car, from when I was four to when I was six. Some nights an emergency or a particularly complicated procedure would keep dad in the hospital for hours after we had arrived, and we sat in the car, playing games like 'guess what I see' until he would come out. Other times we would go to the hospital cafeteria, and there I would see the approving glances from people who knew my dad. They smiled at us and introduced themselves, and a lot of them told me my dad was a great man. I was proud to be his son in those moments. The way people talked to him and how they would listen attentively when he spoke. I liked that too.

His death was ruled an accident, not a suicide. I had no idea what the truth might have been. He was a doctor; surely, he knew what he was doing... but he could also just have been so drunk that he took the wrong amount of sleeping pills. I saw how that could happen, too. I was no stranger to getting so drunk by myself I fell asleep on the kitchen floor. I smoked weed from the moment I woke up to the moment I went to bed just so that I could function. I was more than willing to accept drugs from strangers; I had done it and made some very good friends along the way. I'd never been afraid of people.

I didn't think it mattered in the end whether my dad had done it on purpose or not. What mattered was that he was dead, and I still carried this anvil with me everywhere I went.

It's not like he made it easy to tell him anything. My mom was the one I talked to. But I was a kid, and then she left before the hard part. As a matter of fact, she made things worse. The platitude, the obviousness of it all made me want to vomit.

I'm a slave to something I cannot see.

There was a feeling of static in the air… the colors seemed to come alive in the light coming in from the skylight.

"How can you forgive someone who isn't there anymore?" I asked the empty room.

When I thought about my dad, I felt bitterness and rage, dampened somewhat by dull pervasive grief. I could never ask him anymore, not about my mom or why he had insisted on keeping me when up until that point, he had mostly ignored me. I could never ask if he had made my mom stay away or if she had been happy to leave me behind.

"What am I supposed to do? Bring him back from the dead?"

No reply.

A feeling of urgency overwhelmed me. I was wasting time. Precious, precious time.

8

Nosce te ipsum

Filípa

Filípa stared at her naked body critically in the mirror as she caressed a green and yellow bruise on her left thigh. Water dripped from her hair, and drops rolled down her skin. She felt calmer now. Her body felt comfortable again; she bent her fingers and then stretched down to touch her toes. The heating in the apartment was on to the fullest, so she had a tropical greenhouse in the middle of this northern winter. Her skin wasn't its normal olive tone. It had paled. Her stomach wasn't swollen anymore. She ran her fingers up and down, stopping at the belly button. She then turned her attention to her heart. She used to go into panic attacks when she felt her own pulse. She would try to get out of her body and wiggle until finally, some other sound would get louder, and somehow, she would stop feeling the blood pulsing, coursing, pumping, and she could start breathing again. After years of practice, however, she had learned to seek the heartbeat and to stay with it until it had become familiar, not scary anymore.

She closed her eyes and went to the fingers, where it was easiest to feel the bloody waves breaking against the inside of her body. Breathing in, counting each breath, she stayed. Forcing herself to feel the beat that wouldn't stop. The things keeping her alive were so fragile and, at the same time, so solid. So painful to stop a heart, so hard to drain the blood. *It's impossible to hold your breath until you die,* she thought for some reason.

To feel pain was to be alive. It was tempting, but today she felt like she could get through without it. Filípa went back to looking at her body, searching for the marks he had left on her body. She felt a thrill of exhilaration as she discovered the bite marks like bread crumbs making a path of herself.

She felt unsure as to what to do next. *Warm-up,* she thought, and gingerly grabbed a number two pencil posing it lightly on the rugged surface of the drawing paper. Her hand traced a curved line that little by little became the contour of a face turned three quarters. A woman's delicate features sprouted from her pencil, big eyes, thick mouth, wavy hair. She started carving out the shadows. With each line drawn, her mind relaxed a little, her palms dried up until she could hold the pencil more firmly, then she started working on the eyes: exaggerated lashes, dilated pupils, full mouth half-open. And a hint of teeth. All her drawings ended up looking the same. For someone who took pride in being chameleonic, she was awfully predictable when she was by herself. Somehow, Filípa was only in control when she could make up a character and decide, think as *she,* the character, would.

When alone, it was as if a separate entity took control over which she had no power. When she was sixteen, she had gotten into the habit of making little cuts on her skin, inside the thighs, on her wrists, and with each opening, it was as if a little steam came out. The relief was so immediate.

Her appetite for pain had brought her to BDSM.

During one of their endless evenings in his apartment, Wallace had talked about the topic. He had gone into detail explaining why *Fifty Shades of Grey* was a misrepresentation of BDSM. He explained how women who engage in this kind of sex are not mousy Anastasia Steele types. These women are beings with special needs, unafraid to give up control. They could only fulfill their greatest desires when they were told and shown that they had no option but to let go.

Filípa had already experimented with a little bondage; it was all about being seen while you hid in the shadows. It was about taking those people who have been taught to be obedient and making them do all the things they have always been taught are wrong. It was liberating in a way that she had never tasted before. The first man who had introduced her to this had literally picked her up on the street.

She had been on her way to a *Tinder* date. Filípa was late, and her battery was dying. She managed to pull out the map one last time before the phone died and saw that the bar was somewhere along the big avenue by the train station. She decided she would walk up and down and keep her eyes open for the tall, green-eyed man she was supposed to meet, who had said would be waiting for her by the door of the pub at 11:30 pm.

She walked fast, turning her head and looking around when a tall, green-eyed stranger locked eyes with her. He looked enough like her tinder date so that she held his gaze, and without missing a beat, he walked up to her, a sly, foxlike smile on his face.

"Are you single?" He asked, his hand stretched out to shake hers. She was a little caught off guard, not sure if this was the man she was looking for or some stranger that had seen an opportunity.

"Umm...yes?... Are you… uh… Peter?" The handsome stranger laughed.

"No. But I would like to meet you. Care for a drink?" That moment her survival instinct had kicked in, or perhaps it had been fear, or her mother's voice disguised as good advice, but she turned him down. She turned around to leave, but he grabbed her wrist gently.

"Give me your number," he said.

She hesitated but still gave it to him, half hoping that he wouldn't call. But he did call. She didn't pick up. She figured he would give up after two or three times, and then she wouldn't have to see him. But he persisted and then delivered the final, devastating blow. He sent a text that read:

"Filípa, if you don't want to see me, please tell me, and I will never contact you again."

She felt horrible. Like a little child pretending she didn't hear when people talked to her. She was disgusted with herself and replied, telling him that she *would* see him, to name the time and place. After the appointment was set, she made sure to tell him that she only had one hour to be with him. She told her friend Annalisa from the academy where she was studying to call her after exactly one hour, so she would have an excuse to leave. She was nervous but determined to prove that she was not a coward. And so, she met him in front of the new train station. It was 5:30 in the afternoon.

He was even more handsome than she remembered. Not only tall but broad-shouldered, muscular but not excessively so, with a rugged beard and a wide smile, the kind of picaresque smile that made her legs pop right open. She was drawn to him like a moth to the flame, and he felt it. They ended up in bed together that afternoon, and he introduced her to a world she didn't know existed, a world where she didn't have to be ashamed of wanting to be dominated and *used* by a man with big hands and a big cock who treated her like a rag doll. She couldn't get enough. She let him do anything he asked. Things she would have never dreamt of letting anyone do. Taking pictures of her tangled up in the bedsheets, hair a mess right after being fucked in the ass. Being choked and gagged until the lights went out. Being slapped so hard her ass got red and burned. It felt like she finally understood what people talked about when they talked about sex.

But then, a strange thing happened. The more she gave herself up to him in the bedroom, the less attached to him she was in real life. She realized that she didn't care about him; she wanted nothing else from him but his cock inside her mouth.

His taste in movies bored her, his style was tacky, and while he amused her with his overall slyness and foxlike approach to life, she sensed that they would make each other miserable if they ever pretended that their relationship was anything other than sex. She found him pushy, too. Asking her if she felt anything for him. Telling her he loved her… asking to hold her hand when they walked in the street… She was turned off by it. She wanted the master in the bedroom, and she did not want to reverse the roles in real life. In fact, she wanted nothing to *do* with him in real life.

But he seemed blind to the fact that she was turned off by his personality. He seemed not to notice that her annoyance with him when she was fully clothed was genuine and not some sort of everlasting foreplay. He had to be dealt with as roughly emotionally as she had needed to be dealt with physically. She began spitting bitter words at him, treating him carelessly, canceling their appointments at the last minute, and responding with a loud, unequivocal NO when he asked if she loved him, but he kept trying new tricks to force her to become the girlfriend he wanted instead of the whore she wanted to be.

He refused to fuck her hard and instead told her he wanted to try it 'sweet'. The languid movements and slack-jawed look in his eyes turned her off to the point of nausea. He even began to invite her over and then refuse to have sex with her, claiming he was tired and going to sleep, leaving her stranded in his apartment as buses passed until midnight only, and she could not afford a cab. She didn't like him, but she liked sleeping with him. When the time finally came, she realized what she had to do.

It was easy to leave him in spite of the tears, the never-ending texts, and the empty threats he spat out in the end. She knew they were all just the actions of a proud man who would, nonetheless, accept her decision and eventually back off.

That was when she discovered the power of being selfish. It was a force that said, "*fuck it*," to all the things that she had always been told not to do. But old habits die hard, and sometimes she still found herself running away from the things she wanted the most.

It was hard to fight the voice that told her that she was a fool if she believed that someone could love her. Something inside of her needed to be soothed; she was feeling a deep shame, and she desperately needed someone, anyone, to tell her there was nothing to be ashamed of. And what she had come to realize, little by little, was that that person could be herself.

Fact: she had been economically dependent on her mother until last year.

Fact: she had dropped out of university and did not have a degree.

Fact: she had never had a job for longer than six months.

Conclusion: she was a loser.

But none of it was true. She dropped out of college because she was depressed. She had never had a job for longer than six months because she had been working odd jobs to keep her head up, waitress, call center agent, secretary, but those jobs burned her out; she had to keep changing if she wanted to keep her head together. She was not a loser. She was brave. She was playing basketball with two broken legs. She was playing and trying her hardest. She knew this, yet a part of her brain whispered relentlessly: *you are wasting your time.* She was getting older doing nothing while all her cousins and classmates were getting MBAs.

"Are you sure you need that?" Her mother asked last time she came to visit her as she saw Filípa take a rather high dose of prescribed antidepressants. "You should try jogging. It's so much healthier to release endorphins through exercise than to pump your body full of chemicals. *Here,"* she made a move for the pill Filípa was holding in her hand. Filípa yanked away from her.

"Leave me alone."

Filípa didn't want to start a fight. She closed her eyes, took her pill, and went deep inside herself until her mother's voice sounded like it came from underwater. It was the same with her sister and her father. They didn't understand, and Filípa didn't blame them. She needed to figure out who she was and be reborn since the first version of herself had not worked out, and the people around her couldn't help. Their love, their unconditional yet proud, victim-like love, just made everything worse.

She didn't want blind love; she wanted the love she deserved. If what she elicited was hatred, annoyance, or disgust, then she wanted that too. Anything but the fake smile and "I love you because I have to". She wanted none of it.

Alcohol and weed were not recreational tools for her but emergency rafts. She would hold on to them while her mind swirled at a thousand km per hour in the tempestuous ocean of her thoughts. Without them, she would drown in the whirling dark waters. The joint and the glass of wine were a bunker where she could shelter from the storm until the morning came and she could start all over again.

"*Wait half an hour*," she told herself. "*See if we can make it in half an hour.*"

Time only passed if she forgot about it, if she managed to stop her mind from getting stuck, if she held onto something. Her mind easily raced into a million useless thoughts, repetitions of movie lines, pop songs, past embarrassing moments, redundant mush that gave her nothing and left her with nothing. She was sweating all over from the heat; she turned off the radiator with a brusque gesture.

What she ran away from followed her with weaker echoes. Everything can go two ways. Everything has two sides.

Everything can go either one of two ways, and you get to choose which one.

Why did she run away from Samuel?

A moment of clarity had come when she had been sitting in Samuel's kitchen, soft light entering through the window, the smell of coffee in the air: he was under her skin, and that truth brought a second truth with it:

When the other loves you less than you love them, you are at a greater risk. So, you leave before you are left. That meant Samuel would inevitably leave her sooner or later. In her mind, only men who thought you hated their guts stayed.

She opened the cupboard, took out the plastic glass with her toothbrush, toothpaste, and floss, and meticulously brushed her teeth. Only downward strokes with the upper teeth and vice-versa. And then the tongue. Filípa brushed way back, past her uvula several times, rinsing in between strokes. Finally, she flossed and gargled Listerine.

"I can see why he would think I was in love with him," she said out loud to herself. She was overwhelmed by the desire to be invisible.

Wallace's face appeared in her mind.

She didn't want to be his girlfriend, and she had never expressed or felt any interest in him leaving his wife. He had never accused her of wanting either of those things, yet she could not shake off the impression that he used his mood swings to remind her that she was not part of his life. He kept her at arm's length and treated her coldly because he was afraid of her growing too attached. She hated him for that, but she still did her best to remain cool and aloof. She wanted to prove at all cost that she didn't mind being his mistress; she even relished her role as 'the other woman.'

But the truth was somehow more complicated. She wanted something from Wallace. It seemed something he could easily give her: a little warmth, a little complicity. She wanted to feel he respected her enough to not manipulate her under the excuse that she was too fragile to fall in love with him. She didn't want to be another thing that he had to worry about. She wanted to be a muse, an inspiration, a source of life that would give his already brilliant work yet another level, another dimension. She did her best to be that for him, to be as light as a feather and as soft as a rose. That was what made the sex so good. She was a natural sub, and he was an innate dom.

She felt betrayed whenever he kicked her apart and treated her like another student bothering him for attention. She didn't want a relationship with him, but she thought that if you have seen someone naked and been inside of them, you owe them at least the courtesy of being polite.

Wallace had wanted her from the beginning. The desire was clear from the first moment he had laid eyes on her, or so she had thought. It didn't matter; she had been determined, intoxicated by his brains, his rhetoric, his large and solid presence. He was perfect: older, sophisticated, successful, sexy in a not sexy kind of way. He was in his late fifties, early sixties, with a prominent belly, almost two meters tall with a thick brown and white beard and hairy hands twice the size as hers. When he grabbed her waist, his thumbs almost met at her back. He was heavy, coarse, his body had the distinct smell of older male bodies, not at all unpleasant, but the first time he had laid on top of her, it had shocked her.

She had never been with a man his age before.

It didn't take them long to start sleeping together. One week after classes had started, she had shown up at his house after hours and invited herself in. She had brought the last canvas she had finished with her, a big one, 60 x 45, rolled up under her arm, with the vague excuse of asking him to critique it for her before she presented it for an award. The lamest of reasons, but it had worked. Two bottles of wine and a very charged conversation later, he was sitting next to her on the couch, looking at her, and sliding a hand on her naked thigh. She thought she was going to explode with desire as his hand went up, and up, and up…

He had known what she wanted without her having to tell him. He tied her up with his belt and put his hard cock into her mouth. He turned her over and slapped her; delicious agony washed over her as he twisted her nipple. She was still hooked, attracted to the feeling of being right on the verge of chaos. It made her feel… good? It wasn't a typical kind of good; it was a good intertwined with potential catastrophe and so much sweeter because of it.

Before and after the sex, there was conversation. They talked until words ran out. She liked feeling special; she enjoyed thinking that he had picked *her* out of the litter of students, the anointed one. She liked him, yes, but she knew she would have never enjoyed his hands on her body had it not been for the fact that he held real power over her.

The whole thing felt like a non-reality, like it was happening to someone else, to a character inside her head. A character. Yes. She enjoyed playing the part, but she knew that it wasn't honest in her soul. It was a transaction; she got to feel like a pet, and he got to… what did he get, exactly? Sex, sure. She was young and cute, but if all he wanted was a young pussy, he could have gotten it from a prostitute. She wasn't sure. Sometimes it felt like he actually liked her, and other times it felt like she annoyed him. He could be angry or sweet. He could look at her and make her feel seen or ignore her so completely she felt like her voice had become inaudible. He got something, that was for sure, but she didn't really know what. Perhaps he did it so he could brag about it to his friends. Perhaps he did it because it gave him the thrill to have a secret, or maybe he was just bored. But as much as Filípa would have loved to believe that she was the only one that could have made him transgress the rules like so, she knew it was naive. Just like the reason why she liked him had nothing to do with the actual man, he was attracted to an image he had created around her flesh, not to the flesh itself.

She was so acutely aware of this that she had not even mentioned it to Wallace when he had accidentally impregnated her last year.

Thinking back to that morning when she had taken the test sitting on the toilet of her apartment, she felt numb all over again.

Her castle in the sky had come crashing down like a house of cards that day. She was flesh and blood, a girl, a woman. Which one? She was not a girl, not a teenager. She was closer to thirty than she was to twenty. Yet 'woman' felt like it was still too big of a word, let alone 'Mother'.

At that moment, something had kicked in, an instinct of *self-protection,* and she knew with a calmness that she rarely felt in everyday life that she needed to stop it. It was as if someone more mature and put together had stepped up and said, *all right, child, I'll take it from here.*

Luckily, gratefully, abortion was legal in this northern town. Filípa went to the clinic on a Wednesday morning, hands sweating more than usual, sat on one of the lime green chairs, and waited, while a procession of women came in and out of the doctor's office in various degrees of pregnancy, or with little children holding on to their jeans. She waited patiently, going over the situation in her mind without stopping, considering all the alternative scenarios, and collecting answers for the questions the doctor might ask her.

Finally, they called her name.

Inside, behind a desk with an old PC on it, sat a woman in her fifties, severe-looking, lips pursed and thick-rimmed glasses, conscientiously writing something on a notepad. Filípa stood there, unsure of what to do, waiting for instructions, feeling more miserable with every second that passed. The doctor finally looked up with an expression between exhaustion and exasperation.

She jerked her head and gestured towards the chair with a quick sigh, which Filípa interpreted as a sign that she should sit down. She practically jumped and landed on the plastic chair with metal legs, which made an unpleasant sound against the linoleum floors.

"Date of birth?"

"December 23, 1991."

"When did you get your first menstruation?"

"Thirteen."

"When did you first become sexually active?"

"Eighteen."

"How many sexual partners have you had?"

The doctor looked at her expectantly.

"Eight," she wasn't sure the number was accurate, but her mind had gone blank.

"In the past year?"

Fuck. *Don't sigh, don't roll your eyes.*

"Four."

"Are you on birth control?"

"No."

"Do you use any type of birth control?"

"Condoms."

"Always?"

Clench jaw.

"I try to always use condoms, yes."

"It's a yes or no question."

This time she sighed out loud.

"No, I mean, sometimes things happen—"

"I'm going to need you to be more specific than that. I'm going to need you to tell me all of the occasions on which you had unprotected sex from the time you became sexually active."

Jesus Christ.

She relaxed her shoulders, mustered the sweetest smile she possibly could, and cocked her head a little as she laughed a calculated laugh, not too shrill, not too long, not too loud, and just musical enough.

"I was on birth control, on the pill since I was fourteen. They prescribed it to me for acne problems. I was on it until I was 24, so that's eleven years when I didn't use a condom because I was on the pill. After that, I've only had sex without a condom once because I was drunk, and now we are here."

She smiled her sweet, apologetic smile again and sobbed a bit. The woman was unimpressed.

"Date of your last period."

Now her hands started shaking for real. She really didn't remember. She has always been terrible at keeping track of her cycle. It was never regular to begin with.

She swallowed the ball on her throat.

"I'm not sure." Her voice quivered, but this time it wasn't on purpose.

The doctor was starting to visibly lose her patience.

"Give me one second, please," she said and couldn't help but notice how her accent sounded thicker this time around.

Wallace had never used a condom when they were together. The conversation had never come up. Somehow, she had convinced herself that if he hadn't brought it up, perhaps it was thanks to having had a vasectomy or something, but she also never asked. She ignored the fact that he always came on her belly and wrote it off as his personal preference. When she found she was pregnant, she felt lonelier than ever before in her entire life.

She was afraid he would make her keep it. She was afraid he would be angry with her. She was afraid of his wife, of his children. She was afraid he would blame her, judge her, think that she had done it on purpose to tie him down. No. It was better to keep her head down, smile, and get the whole thing over with as little pain as possible.

She had an app on her phone that helped her keep track of her period, but the wheels were only now beginning to turn in her head: When she was under pressure, her mind reacted ten times slower, like a deer in the headlights, she froze.

With slippery fingers, she took out her android, put in the code wrong twice, opened the wrong app, closed it, and finally, there it was, Flo. Her heart raced as she realized she had not updated the information since the beginning of the year.

She looked at the dates with a dry mouth and gave one that seemed accurate.

The doctor looked at her as a disappointed mother, sighed, and wrote something down.

"We'll do an ultrasound," she said.

The hospital was big, and she got lost twice before she found the right ward. They gave her two pills. She stayed all day at the hospital. The pain was terrible but no worse than the worst cramp she had ever had. And then it was over. She was the master of her body again. A little sadness came more from feeling so alone, but she was mostly relieved. She met Wallace again a few weeks after, and she did not say a word.

She knew it was better that way.

9

One of two ways

Filípa

When she woke up, the apartment was cold. Filípa went over to check the radiator, her stomach curling as her naked feet touched the tiled floor. It was dead. Stumbling, she made her way into her bedroom and dived under the stone-cold sheets, her mind swirling in a fog.

Why was she suddenly afraid? There was nothing to be afraid of. She was a person. She had a house. No one was trying to hurt her. Why did she keep seeing monsters everywhere she looked?

She sat up and sat cross-legged on the bed, not ignoring the cold but diving into it, adjusting to it, until she didn't shiver anymore, felt her heart rate slow down. She breathed and repeated the same words over and over, focusing on the cold air on the tip of her nose whenever her mind derailed into obscure fantasies. Soon, the world halted. *I am here*, she said, and felt the sheets under her legs, watched the paint peeling on the ceiling, the veins on the wooden beams. She felt the weight of her body against the mattress, the roar of the river, and the voices on the street. *I exist in a place.* She breathed again. *Nobody is hunting me.* She closed her eyes.

I am an animal of prey. A rabbit, a deer. I am prey. They can smell me. Some people are predators, and some people are prey. But no, that wasn't quite right. She had been a predator too; she simply preferred the guiltless role of the prey.

She got out of bed, a little animal sniffing the air.

Filípa looked into the full-length mirror on the wall opposite to her bed and scratched her scalp; it was dirty, dandruff fell on the covers.

Hungry. She was hungry. Her stomach churned; acid lapped her esophagus. The rumbling was almost unbelievable in its loudness. But she couldn't eat. Five days of a steady diet of kebabs and beer had left her wounded. Her stomach was bloated, and it felt like a billion tiny needles were poking her intestines. It was her usual unease.

Things that ought to scare me out, don't, and things that shouldn't, do. She kept seeing giants where there were only windmills while the real monsters went by unnoticed.

As a child, every night before bed, she would ardently recite the prayer of the Angel of God, mouthing the words with her eyes shut tight, putting all the strength she had behind each word to protect her from evil.

It was scary to think of countless things that threatened her little world. Everything was always a second away from disappearing, yet somehow, nothing ever changed.

It was 2:45 am.

Alone in her room, it was Samuel's sweet smile that made her feel better, not Wallace's animal roughness.

"Sam," she found herself whispering, longing for his long fingers and his soft skin. "Samuel, Samuel, Samuel." She repeated his name like a spell, over and over, until suddenly, she knew.

She knew what she had to do.

PART II

10

Lockdown

Samuel

June 2020

Who could have ever predicted that a global pandemic would affect me this much? I mean, I hardly ever left my house anyway. I hated people. I was socially isolated before it was cool to socially isolate.

Yet it was during that weird time that I found myself completely obliterated by the presence of another person. This was not a bad thing. I loved watching her be. Filípa.

She followed the seasons.

With March and the light rains of spring, her smile began to surface more, and a sort of melancholic sweetness overcame her.

In the warmth of the summer, as her skin toasted and she shed layers of clothing, a bubbly side of her emerged that I hadn't seen before. Joy started to take over, and our house was suddenly in technicolor.

Filípa was quiet to the point of awkwardness, and I could almost see the instant in which she would put her mind on autopilot and withdraw into a place deep inside herself, where not even I could reach her. She was a good actress though, and you had to *watch* her for you to see that she wasn't really there.

With the sun, more things about her came to light.

"I got to a point where I realized this isn't going away," she told me one day over glasses of red wine. "I thought my anxiety was *place-related,*" she went on. "But I realized after two years that *it* is not going anywhere that I don't go, that I have to find some way to live with it. If I let this thing win, I'm really gonna get to a point where I won't be able to do anything on my own."

I nodded, 65% sure of what she was talking about.

"Look," she said and put up her palms. "See?" I touched her open palm. "They're not sweating," she explained and laughed from her belly. "They used to sweat all the time, no matter where I was or what I was doing. I used to be ashamed of shaking people's hands or holding hands with a boy. I thought they would think I was gross. They told me that it was a condition and I would have to live with it my whole life," she held her palm up to mine, caressing it. "They don't sweat anymore."

While the world outside was burning, we had created our own inside my father's house. The first one to wake up would go downstairs, play a record, and make coffee. If I woke up first, I would sometimes cook. Little by little, I was getting her to eat a piece of toast or a bowl of cereal instead of the endless stream of coffee and cigarettes that she usually had for breakfast. Then, depending on whether we had something to do or not, we would either go back to bed or to the shower. Or sometimes, she would lock herself up in my father's studio and sketch while I read stuff online. She liked grocery shopping and enjoyed cooking, even if she wasn't very good at it, and had a tendency to over-salt things. Whenever I wanted to cook something a little more complicated for dinner and enlisted her help, she was always game and performed whatever task I gave her conscientiously, to the point of obsession. The carrots had to be cut into perfect cubes, the garlic had to be minced into a powder. She seemed to enjoy the praise I gave her when she completed a task correctly. She looked as happy as a schoolgirl who had been given a gold star on an assignment. She was childlike in many ways; her curiosity and fascination over even the most trivial domestic tasks were sincere. Nonetheless, when she was angry or sad, she looked a million years older, her gaze became cold, and I felt frightened. Her tongue could be sweet or acid, and I was learning, little by little, just what made her tik.

She reminded me of a raccoon sometimes, the way she took things in between her tiny hands and turned them around to examine them. She amused me. She had taken over the cleaning and bought new supplies to replace the empty bottles on my shelf. She scrubbed the shower and got rid of the lines of mold that I had become so used to. I was surprised when I saw them gone. She always washed the dishes right after we ate and, for some reason, refused to use the dishwasher. She had a fixation with bugs but, just like me, she didn't kill the spiders.

"*It's bad luck*," she told me matter-of-factly when I pointed it out.

As the weather grew warmer, she got into the habit of walking around the house in nothing but panties. The more naked she was, the more she seemed herself, a girl happy in her own skin, as guarded and self-contained as she had seemed before, she seemed to have shifted somehow, and all that sadness and confusion that had been pouring out of her before now transformed into some sort of savage joy and untamed sexiness that had almost nothing to do with the body itself. I could feel a change happening in me too. I could feel that somehow, all the things that seemed so heavy before didn't really matter anymore. For the first time in a long time, I didn't feel defeated before starting the race.

It seemed that all I had to do was touch her, and she would get so wet between the legs I couldn't believe it. Her mouth would hang half-open, she would moan, and I could feel myself almost bursting with desire. Her mouth was always open for me.

We were both careful about what we asked and told each other. I guess we were both subconsciously trying to keep up the game as long as possible, to keep living in that pleasant cloud of borrowed time.

I don't know how long we thought it would last, if it would last forever or be over in the blink of an eye. Neither one of us was looking forward; we were both in a forever stretching *now*. We were living at our own rhythm, in our own space and time.

A wise man would have told me it could not last forever, but I despised wise men. Let them keep their wisdom. *If they are right, I'll find out.*

We could both sense that there were painful spots in our minds that were still too tender to be touched, but I could sense *her*; I somehow knew that there was someone who also knew the depths.

I could see that her own heart puzzled her, and I never pressured her for explanations or information. In return, she did the same for me. Free from the baggage, we could start fresh, to be no one but whoever we wanted to be when we were together, and there was no need to pretend. We both seemed to understand that this was a rare place to be. To be disarmed in front of someone and, at the same time, be safe.

11

Nosce te Ipsum II

Samuel

Previous relationships had been on my mind lately.

There had been Silvia, whom I met when I was fourteen and went on to be with until I was twenty-four. She was my first girlfriend and also the first woman I lived with. We grew up together, and by the end, it was hard to remember the reason why it had all started in the first place.

She hated her parents as much as I hated my parents, and we moved in together when we were eighteen, so we could be away from them. I got a job as a low-level computer programmer at a bank. I had learned the basics in high school, plus I had always loved computers, so I had learned a lot on my own. I enrolled in university, but it wasn't long before life got too overwhelming, and I dropped out. Silvia opened a jewelry store with a loan we got together, but after three years, her efforts fizzled, and the debts started piling up.

People who say money doesn't buy happiness have never been in the position of counting change to pay the gas bill. We finally broke up, and she went back to living with her parents. At least, gas bills were covered over there.

After Silvia, a long stream of prostitutes and one-night stands followed. I wanted sex, not a relationship. Then there was Sophie, and now Filípa.

I looked at her. She was lying naked on my bed. Her hips were a hill that folded into her waist and then up again. The nipples were erect like the flag explorers put on the top of mountain peaks.

I ran my fingers all the way from her toes to the top of her head. She shuddered.

I felt old. I had felt old for most of my life, but looking at Filípa I realized, almost with a shock, that I wasn't. I was thirty. Nobody but a sixteen-year-old would have called me anything but a young man. In fact, the way things were going, I probably still had ten good years ahead of me for being young, or at least for being thought of as young.

"You look younger than you are," I said to Filípa as she opened her eyes and smiled sleepily at me.

"People tell me that a lot," she replied.

"Do you feel young?"

"I don't know if the way I feel is the way people feel when they say they feel young."

She furrowed her brow and chewed the inside of her cheek, as she always did when she was trying to find the right words to express herself.

"I don't really know what feeling young is. I mean, I know rationally that I'm young. Mathematically, statistically, I am part of the population that is referred to as young, but I remember being fifteen and feeling that I was old. I remember thinking that it was already too late for me to take up basketball, that it was too late to get into martial arts. Those were the things people began when they were kids. If you wanted to be really good, you had to start young, otherwise why bother? I was already fifteen."

"You should start now," I said rather stupidly.

She shook her head.

"No, that's not my point. My point is that I feel younger now than I did when I was fifteen, so whatever feeling young is, it has nothing to do with age."

Filípa bit her lip and laughed bitterly.

"I don't remember being a happy child, and I have tried really hard during my twenties to forget my adolescence. I remember those years… I tainted them with a tinge of gray. I remember wanting to not wake up the next morning. The depression might have begun when I was thirteen, but the term was not in my vocabulary. Children don't get depressed, right? By the time I was sixteen, I had found it difficult to breathe. I didn't know it was possible to get out of that state where everything felt like it weighed a thousand kilos... I thought everyone was making fun of me… I thought anyone I let get close to me would hurt me. I was *too much something.* Too ugly, too quiet, too chatty, or too weird. One girl once told me she simply didn't like the sound of my voice. I'm not sure exactly why, after all these years, I'm not sure why they decided that I was the one marked for high school misery." She giggled nervously, then went on. "If you are at the top of the food chain, I can see how it must have been fun. High school, I mean. I can see how it must have been easy to turn away from the girl everyone had decided was a social pariah. I was just sad. I was sad, and then I was nothing. One day, after a particularly heinous experience, I realized that I didn't even feel hurt anymore, that I felt nothing. I was transparent, invisible, unimportant, and that somehow made me feel relieved."

Filípa grew silent.

"I'm making it sound more dramatic than it was," she said, finally, with a laugh and a shrug.

I didn't say anything but waited. I knew that she sometimes took long pauses to gather her thoughts. I knew she liked to be clear about what she meant and that it was sometimes hard for her.

"It was more like a general indifference," she went on. "I could go for entire days without speaking a word. After a while, I assumed something was wrong with me, that I was wired the wrong way. People seemed to be on a different frequency like my brain was in AM, and everyone was tuned to FM. After I left, I never talked to a single person, and I never wanted to, either. It was as if all those people who have been extras in my life since I was five years old. I tried really hard to forget, to never go back. I refused to believe there was something inherently wrong with me, and instead, I blamed the place. I left, and I never looked back and, in a way, I think has defined my life forever. Seven years later, when I didn't hand in my thesis and failed to graduate from college, a part of me wondered if I had been following a pattern, unconsciously repeating the actions of the past, for I felt somehow comfortable in the misery of being a failure... but the thing is, it never felt like a choice. One day I woke up, and it was two years later; I was too late to graduate, too late to start a new thesis, too late to go back to school, too late for everything. I gave up again. I decided that the way for me was to try to be as little of a burden as possible to those around me. After two years of watching me lie about writing the thesis and living off the money she sent me every month at the place she was paying for me, my mother had reached the end of her rope. It got to a point where I knew if I didn't get a job and get out of that place, we were both gonna go crazy. Crazier. So, I went to a call center, and three hours later, I had a job. The thesis, university, mother, and family, nothing seemed quite as important. I discovered that graduating from a university was not the most interesting thing someone could do. For the first time, I was making money, partying, drinking the second the shift was over, and waking up the next day to do it all over again. For a while, it was lovely. It was freedom."

She kept going, her speech falling into a pattern, flowing more easily now.

"I discovered how much men liked me. I was popular for the first time, and I loved it. I wasn't afraid anymore, and whether something had changed in me or in everyone else, we all now seemed tuned into a closer frequency."

She spoke like this sometimes and then caught herself, laughed at her own words, and made some self-deprecating remark to make it clear that she was half-joking, that she didn't actually believe half the shit she was saying, but the truth was, I saw right through her. It was obvious to me how much she enjoyed talking and opening up and putting feelings into words, and spiking reality with imagination to make the real world less dull, and I didn't care that much about the truth to begin with.

12

Of Monsters and Men

Filípa

She watched the sheet fall slowly on the mattress, deflating as the air from underneath seeped out from between the cotton threads, how the perfect tent flattened into a flawless rectangle as the edges of the sheet fell over the edges of the mattress. She ran her hand over the sheet to smooth it over until it was wrinkle-less. The weather was getting warmer. The nights had been so cold she had been wearing three pairs of socks under the thick duvet, and though she still wore socks to bed, the duvet had been put away.

There was something satisfying about rearranging her closet at the end of each season, to put away the thick clothes and bring out the lighter ones, to dust all the places where objects and other invisible things had gathered during the winter.

Samuel was quickly becoming her best friend, which was new since she had never been friends with the men she was sleeping with.

Men are different creatures. She had been taught they were both the strong protectors *and* the vile creatures who would hurt a girl just because. As she grew older, she had unconsciously begun to think of them as alien to her, creatures who were smart for the world they had created but ultimately unable to understand the depths of a woman's soul, simple creatures who could not possibly begin to grasp the massive, complex web of emotions that laid inside of her.

Since the time she was a little girl, adult women gave her a warning: men want only one thing from you. Be careful of them.

I was taught to run away when I saw a man coming towards me on the street. I was also taught to yell my father's name while I ran to let him know that I had men to protect me, that I wasn't a girl alone.

It was a strange conundrum, this dichotomy between being afraid of men and also seeking them for protection.

From that point of view, there were two types of men in the world: On one side, her father, her uncles, her grandfather, her cousins, who were the 'good men'. On the other side, the hordes of invisible, mindless apes that waged war and got into fist fights and abused women and wanted to take advantage of little girls just like her.

She had gotten tired of being afraid of men, so she had made it a point to prove that she wasn't. She went out and went up to men, and it was easy, so easy to get them to buy her a drink and give her attention. Sometimes she slept with them, but sometimes she didn't. She realized very quickly that there was nothing to be afraid of. Men were neither flawless protectors nor mindless apes; they were just people, and to understand a person, all you had to do was observe. She learned to efface herself, and while at first this felt like freedom, it was only another trap.

She hid her true face and created another face for the world to see, keeping her inner world her own. Little by little, she began to blur the lines between real emotion and created emotion until she had no clue whether what she was feeling was a genuine reaction to a situation or a clever ruse of her own making. Self-deception was a helpful tool when reality got too painful. But it was a lie.

Things that are big and heavy should be given their due weight. Trying to mask painful things with forced joy made them grotesque.

After her parent's messy divorce, for example, everyone kept insisting that things were better now, that this was all a change for the good when it was so clearly not at all true.

She felt like she was going insane. She played along. She smiled. She fiercely supported her mother in her decision to leave the house in front of her aunts, who all gave her proud looks of approval. She condemned her father in her heart, even if she diligently continued to see him when he called. She took her mother's side, even if this was also never spoken because the other part of the charade was that her mother pretended that she had zero resentments against her father and that everything he had ever done had been for her and her sister's good even if their marriage had not worked, he was the best father any daughter could ever ask for, and she should be grateful for him. That's what she would *say*. But her mother's voice took a bitter tone when she talked about him. And the person she most talked to was Filípa herself. Filípa had to listen to her, to agree, and then go out and pretend that she hadn't.

Her father, who had barely put up a fight when her mother had decided that she had full custody of her and her sister. Her father, who had put all the weight of responsibility of the separation on her mother's shoulders. Her father, who made Filípa feel excruciatingly guilty because she, *the child,* hadn't chosen him in the fight. She hoped her father would understand that she couldn't leave her mother since that would destroy her, but her father, her ever shy and unsure father, had not understood.

When he asked her if she wanted to live with him, it felt so awkward, and the atmosphere got so charged so fast inside the car that she panicked. She couldn't tell her mother that she had chosen to live with her father. That would have meant she wanted to leave her, and that was a betrayal. She was her mother's ally. She needed her father to leave her no choice, but in his graciousness, he kept treating her like an adult when she was a scared child of fourteen who thought her mother would crumble to the ground if she left her.

But she couldn't say any of it. Because none of what was happening was that big of a deal. Everyone was adamant in keeping up a smile, and no one ever told her the one thing she really needed to hear:

This shit has not been easy. You are not a selfish piece of shit for feeling the way you feel.

She allowed herself to cry only when her mother and her sister allowed themselves to cry. She only let the tears spill when they were sitting around a round table in the small apartment her mother had rented for the three of them to live in while the big house was sold. All of her relatives on her mother's side had helped transport furniture and boxes to the new place. Everyone had tried hard to keep a sunny atmosphere, cracking jokes, moving, carrying, hurrying, grunting, never a moment of silence. It actually did seem like it was just another move, a move to another apartment, a new adventure, the beginning of a new life, but the second the door shut behind the back of the last guess, the heaviness fell. They all realized that this was not a beginning but a strange sort of limbo. In this passing place, they would have to figure out how to live as women without men, daughters without a father, and a wife with no husband.

Something had cracked. The eggshell had broken. Filípa was no longer a kid who believed adults were somehow surer than she was of what they were doing. She had seen her mother cry and her father drink; she had seen the lie in everybody's smile. She could not go back to believing that grownups would make everything all right.

She was a grown-up now, and she had the chance to do things differently. Filípa was a lot of things, but she was not a coward, and only cowards repeat the same mistakes twice.

Right?

13

Ghosts

Filípa

Wallace's message flashed on the screen. He was pulling out the big guns in her attempt to lure her back. He was not apologetic but remorseful, full of promises and adulation. She knew. She knew *him.*

She had not told Wallace that she was living with Samuel. She had not told him about the abortion. She had not said anything for months. But twistedly, that was how their relationship worked. He called and she came.

He was still married, of course.

There had never been a real relationship, and she wasn't into whatever it was anymore, but she couldn't bring herself to end it. Looking at the message on her screen, a part of her wondered if perhaps she should keep him on the sidelines, just in case. It wasn't fair to Samuel, but then again, she hadn't cheated on him. She hadn't answered the message, but she felt guilty already; in her mind, she was already trying to justify the potential faux pas… if he ever found her out, of course. She remembered her parents. Why had her parents broken up? She wasn't sure. For all of her rants, her mother had never actually given a concrete explanation. Filipa had surmised that there hadn't really been a reason, not a concrete one, just the accumulation of years and years lacking real love, the unhappy ending to an unhappy union that left the two people who had formed it a little different, their souls molded by the weight of living every day hoping that the person sleeping next to you will somehow be able to give you what you need, without the cumbersome business of actually having to tell them.

It still surprised her how little her parents seemed to know about each other, how much they had hidden. Who knows how many secrets they had, they shared, they hid? Now that she was no longer a child, she realized she didn't want to know. Leave them alone with their secrets. People have a right to them. Even parents.

But as a kid, the truth is, she felt perpetually alone.

Filípa looked back at the message on her phone.

"*What about Samuel?*" said a voice inside her head.

As a teenager, she had fiercely rebelled against anything and everything that had the faintest scent of enforced normalcy. She was still sad, but now she was also angry, and the surrounding people, if they noticed, remained quiet. She rebelled, she yelled that she was against everything they stood for, and the world answered with deafening silence.

Not that she was all that loud, to begin with. Both her anger and her sadness were directed towards the inside. Filipa, as angry as she was, did not, in the end, want to hurt anyone, not even anything. The only thing that she wished for, secretly, ardently, silently, was to slowly but surely become invisible and disappear.

And then there was the Academy, and Wallace.

Boy, oh boy, was that a whole new world. She had never felt chic or sophisticated; the world where people talked about art and things ethereal had always seemed almost like fiction, a fantasy. Before coming to this northern town, a part of her still found it hard to believe that there were people out there in the world who could actually, seriously dedicate themselves fully and completely to something as silly and seemingly useless as painting. In her broken mind, only things that were practical and mechanical had any value; if she could have chosen how to be born, she would have asked to be really good at math so that she could have become an engineer, or a software programmer, or a scientist, or someone how could make a difference, she would have given anything to swap her dreamy, soft, colorful mind for something made out of nuts and bolts, of still, something mechanical that could produce something other than doodles and daydreams.

Filipa was very much aware of the fact that this strange self-hatred had to come only from herself. Her parents had always encouraged and supported her. Then, what had gone wrong? She didn't know. What she did know was that feeling of emptiness, that cold dread that started at the pit of her stomach and then swallowed her from the inside out and left her unable to move. It was shame, mixed with sadness, mixed with loneliness, that unnameable nothing that told her one thing and one thing only: you don't belong.

She had never belonged. Not with anyone, not anywhere. Definitely not at school. Kids her age seemed to despise her. Since she was five, she had been haunted by this feeling of being different, and it was not good. Whenever she heard the phrase 'be yourself', which was used pervasively in all ads during the '90s and early 2000s, she wanted to cry because who she was, was clearly wrong. They had made her wrong. Too sweet, too naive, too smart for her own good, good at useless things, useless at useful ones. Filípa had always felt like too much of the wrong things.

Until the Academy.

There, she had felt okay. She was the regular. Too regular, even. People didn't call her weird because everyone was weird. She didn't have to stop and think if what she was doing was crazy or not because everyone else was on the same boat. People talked seriously about how art made them feel, and it wasn't ironic or a mockery. Here she could be moved to tears by a painting, and she didn't have to be afraid of people making fun of her for it. Here, she was okay. She belonged. In this northern town, part of this northern country, people could afford to care about beautiful things.

And there was Wallace.

Having him had felt like the culmination of everything she had always wanted. He gave her value; he made her feel seen. Countless hours she had spent fantasizing about the amazing life she would have as his muse, his mistress, his oasis of freedom that he would come to when the load of being himself got too heavy, and she would be waiting for him, fabulous and thin, wrapped in a gorgeous silk shawl, in her little studio apartment downtown that he helped pay for, of course, so that she could spend hours cultivating her body and her mind, and painting freely, of course, without any pressure, whatsoever, to actually have to sell a thing. A part of her resisted the fantasy, even back then. A part of her, probably the last remnant of sanity within her, told her that she was serving herself like food.

What is evil if not *not caring*?

What makes people good if not their innate desire to treat others with dignity?

When we stop caring, we lose. When we assume love is sturdy, impermeable, set when in reality, love is an ecosystem, a live terrarium that you have to nurture and take care of, because it is as fragile as it is beautiful.

He doesn't have to know, another voice in her head answered. Her heart thumped inside her ribcage as she typed quickly and hit send before she could think about it enough. *There*, she thought. His reply came almost immediately, which was weird for him. He must have really missed her.

Meet me at the Plaza.

He was already waiting for her when she arrived at the Plaza Café. He looked exactly how she expected him to look, yet somehow completely different, older, a bit unknown. She had made an effort to look good for him; and walked towards the table.

It was an unusually sunny day.

"You look great."

His compliment embarrassed her; she felt her cheeks blush.

"Thank you, it's my real hair," she blabbered out and felt immediately stupid.

"I didn't think it was a wig," he replied with a funny smile. He had stood up to greet her and made a move to kiss her, but she avoided his face. It was very awkward. With an apologetic laugh, they both sat down at the little table close to the heater.

"How are you?" He asked.

"I'm fine. How are you?"

He sighed.

"I'm fine. I'm glad to be with you. I've missed you."

For some reason, this made her angry.

"How's your wife?" She shot back.

"It's not much of a marriage, you know that." He said gravely, not at all amused.

Silence.

"Wallace, I- I've been seeing someone. I'm living with him. He is good for me. He is- he seems to like me."

Why was her tone so sheepish? What the hell did she have to apologize for?

Wallace smiled at her sweetly.

"Filípa, who wouldn't like you? He is a lucky guy. I'm happy for you."

It felt as if a huge weight had been lifted off her shoulders, and she relaxed. She was now glad to see him. She liked him as a person. Leaning back on her chair, she pulled out a cigarette, and they started to talk.

The waiter came and took their order. Two Caesar salads and a bottle of Barbera. Soon, the 14% grade wine started to take its toll, and time began to dilate. The conversation flowed, the second bottle was opened, and it was easy and elevating somehow. Talking to him always made her feel smarter, classier, like she could be a famous painter someday, like she was actually talented enough to be noticed by the notoriously closed-off art world. She loved to paint, she had always loved to, but she wasn't foolish enough not to realize that she wasn't any better, or any worse, than the millions of others who wanted to be the lucky, the special one, that got to live off her art. But with Wallace, with the wine, that feeling came back, a feeling that encompassed all of her ambition into one cocktail of sensation. The sun was going down. Who knew how many hours had gone by when Wallace, looking at her through the now-empty wine bottle, said in that low baritone that she had always found so alluring:

"You want to move this to my place?"

No, she thought. I should say no. I should go back to Sam.

Behind the fog of the wine, the other voice quickly gave her an option:

He doesn't have to know. Besides, we're just going to his house to keep on talking. Nothing has to happen. I can handle this.

Ha!

Samuel

I saw her, but she didn't see me. It was late afternoon, and she had told me she had an appointment with one of her friends from the Academy. She walked fast, oblivious to the other pedestrians, hands in pockets, brow furrowed, moving like a serpent amongst the sea of people walking in the opposite direction. I tried to call her, but she didn't look at her phone. She was wearing headphones, I saw. I followed her. She looked like she didn't want to be seen.

She slithered through the crowd, got on the train, and I got in after her, through a different door, careful to stay out of her field of vision. She wasn't looking around anyway. Her face was stony as she looked straight out the clear glass doors of the tram, not once turning her head, even though I wasn't the only male burning holes into her back.

I wondered if any of the other men looking at her ass had, like me, actually touched it. The thought turned me on and made me jealous at the same time. The doors opened, and she got down from the bus, oblivious to the fact that she had just been the protagonist of a very elaborate sexual fantasy. I followed her out like a shadow.

She went into a bar, and my stomach sank as I saw her "friend" was an older man. At first, she seemed tense, but he got close to her little by little. His hand slithered to her thigh. I wanted to stop looking, but I couldn't. I wanted to jump up and confront her, but I didn't. I waited, cradling my vodka tonic and staring at them immobile and silent. After a couple of hours, they left together, and through my drunken gaze, I swear I saw her turn her head towards me and smile an evil little smile.

14

Contrition

Filípa

Filípa already regretted going to Wallace's apartment at the moment she arrived. She hadn't wanted to, but it was almost as though she couldn't refuse to him. She was prey of the worst kind of pleasure: the joy of a slave who has won their master's favor and proves it in her own flesh, and the calm of a dog following its owner.

Her relationship with Samuel had changed her. She had simply failed to see until now how deep her chains went, how deeply prejudiced she was against herself and those like her, and how utterly afraid she was to be a alone in the world that she would let men use her to mitigate the fear and keep the shadows at bay.

When she was little, she thought beauty was all a woman needed. She wasn't stupid; she was a clever kid. She saw how the beautiful women were thrown into the limelight while those deemed ugly by the almighty patriarchy were cast into the shadows: the ugly, the old, the poor, and the intelligent ones.

When she was little, and for a long time after she had stopped being little, she had fought tooth and nail for a spot in the limelight, torturing herself over every extra calorie consumed, belittling other women to get ahead of herself, straightening her hair so it would look more like Hanna Montana's, less like hers, buying expensive makeup that she could not afford because the ads promised her everything that she had always craved: Love and acceptance.

But it was only now, lying in this older man's bed that she understood how wrong her approach had been. She shouldn't have fought for a spot in any fucking limelight; she was meant to be the light itself.

She had felt remorse at the moment she'd laid down next to him in bed and he touched her breasts, his weight over her like a storm cloud and her knees easing apart.

"Stop," she said.

"What?"

"I said, stop."

"Are you okay, Filipa?"

"No, I'm not."

She sat up and hugged her knees, feeling an unbearable cold emptiness within her chest, the same that had been chasing her since she was five. Wallace tried to touch her, but she recoiled. The silence was charged, electric.

"Did you ever love me?" The words were difficult to say, but her voice sounded steady. She realized she had wanted to ask him that for a long, long time.

"What is even love? One could wonder—"

"Don't take that patronizing tone with me, please. For once, just tell me the truth. What were you even doing with me? What was I to you?"

Wallace sighed and looked down. For a second, he seemed much, much older. It was as if a veil had been lifted, and she suddenly saw him for what he was: an old, tired, naked man.

"I…" he cleared his throat. "I don't know." Even his voice sounded different to her. A chill went up to her spine. He continued with a defeated smile on his face. "You were you. You have something, Filipa. Something that everyone in the world can see, except for you. A force, a wildness, mixed in with a wise melancholy that was just impossible to resist. I had never actually had a full-blown affair before. I don't know if I ever loved you, but I certainly wanted something from you."

"What?" Her voice was barely a whisper.

He smiled and gently stroked her cheek.

"To see the world through your eyes. To see *myself* through your eyes. You were sincere. In this world full of bullshit, you were genuine, authentic. I've lost that now."

"So, you used me." Her voice acquired a harsh tone.

"We used each other. The difference is that I was chasing something real while you were chasing a lie."

Filípa considered it and looked back at him. He was telling the truth. What she had wanted from him was his approval, his validation, but she noticed that she had had it to begin with, for years, but it hadn't mattered in the slightest: nobody's approval or validation would. Nobody's approval would matter besides her own damn self's.

And she thought of Sam. She had betrayed him. She had already hurt him, perhaps irreparably.

Wallace offered to call her a cab, but she declined. She left his apartment, walking slowly towards the bus stop. It was almost an hour's ride to Sam's house.

She wanted to cry but couldn't. She needed to be strong for what was coming.

15

Velvet Bullets

Samuel

I went back home, hating myself; I wrote one message after another. The two checkmarks appeared, but they didn't turn blue. I waited for Filípa sitting in the dark of the living room, only the foot lamp on, its amber light giving my skin a reddish tone. I smoked, and I waited. When she finally came in the front door, I could smell the other man on her.

"Hey."

"Hey."

"It's late."

"I know."

I could hear a ticking clock. Was there a clock in the house? Where?

"Where were you?"

Let's play, I thought.

"I… I told you, I met an old friend."

"Aha. Anybody I know?"

"No, not really. I'm sorry I didn't reply to your messages, my phone had like 3% battery left and—"

"I saw you."

Her face fell.

"Sam, I…" Her voice caught in her throat. I waited for her to keep on talking, but all I could hear was that goddamn clock.

"Yes?"

"What did you see?"

Coward.

"Are you gonna make me tell you?"

"Sam, I'm sorry. I'm so sorry… nothing actually happened, I—"

"So, you didn't sleep with him."

'I stopped it before it actually happened, but Sam—"

"What?" I could hear the anger in my voice.

She sobbed.

"I'm sorry, I'm so sorry, I don't know, I didn't realize—"

"You didn't *realize*? What exactly? What the fuck does that even mean?"

"It was like... I was a different person. I've been different since I've been with you; I feel better when I'm with you."

I felt sick.

"So, you had to go and fuck some old guy? What for? Who was he?"

"My old teacher. I had a relationship with him before… well, it wasn't really a relationship; it was more like a… I don't even know what it was. Sam, please—"

"I thought we had a good thing going. I was happy. I'm such an idiot."

"No, no, you aren't. I'm the idiot. A perfect asshole. You—When I'm with you, I feel closer to myself. With him I was trying to be someone else; I was trying to be that bad bitch who doesn't care about anything… but I'm not that. I'm just me, and you see me… please don't stop seeing me."

"I don't understand you."

"I don't understand me."

She shook her head, covered her face, and finally broke down and cried.

I wanted to kill her. I would have happily kicked her in the gut, for real this time. I was humiliated. I thought I knew her; in my idiocy I thought that we had been on the same page, that we were in some sort of alternate dimension where only the two of us existed. Like a fireball, rage shot up my body, and I punched the wall so hard the paint chipped and my skin cracked open.

Filípa was curled up into a ball on the ottoman chair she liked best. Her huge eyes stared unblinkingly, shiny. She reached out to me, but I slapped her hand away. I could feel the rage inside me, pulsing.

"Sam," she whispered, and the sound of her voice just made me angrier.

“No,” I said, taking deep breaths.

She slowly got up and tried to get near me again, but I put my arm between us.

“Stay away from me.”

Her eyes filled with tears again.

“Sam, I beg you. I’m so sorry. I know now. I want you. I choose you.”

“You don’t get to ‘choose’ me.” I spat. “And besides, you had to fucking sleep with someone else to realize that you want to be with me? That’s one hell of a litmus test Filípa. Go to him, go get fucked by someone else. I don’t want you in my house. I don’t want to see your fucking face.”

She looked like a child, small, lost, frightened.

“But what I’m I supposed to do? Where am I supposed to go?”

“I don’t care what you do. Just get out of my house.”

“No.”

“What the fuck do you mean no? This is my house, bitch, and if I tell you to leave, you fucking leave, got it?”

She stood up with a new fire alight in her eyes.

“No.”

I could feel my blood pulsing through my skin.

“Filípa, I swear to god, either you get out or I—"

“What? You what? You’ll hit me? Go ahead, hit me! Do you think I’m afraid of you?”

I *wanted* to hit her. I wanted to hurt her. I had never wanted to hurt anyone so bad in my life, not my father, not my mother, or Sophie. Instead, I took the couch and flipped it over. It fell on the record shelf, breaking the glass, ruining more than a few precious pieces of vinyl as they dropped on the hardwood floor, the record player shattering underneath the wreckage. Filípa looked at me from the corner of the room, knees bent, fists clenched, eyes on me, attentive, ready to fight me, if necessary, even if we both knew I would have destroyed her. She knew if I chose to, I could have hurt her, and still, she faced me, not ashamed, not afraid, not even small anymore. She stood tall, ready for anything.

I wanted to leave the house. I wanted to run, and keep on running, and forget her face, erase her forever, go back to that winter night under the streetlamp and ignore the stranger beside me, not to be so dumb as to invite some stranger into my life just because I was feeling lonely.

But mostly, I realized, I was tired. Exhausted, sad, and lonely; the rage seeped out of me like water through a strainer. I fell on my knees, my arms hanging like noodles on my sides.

I had thought that such a thing was impossible and that all the doubts were only in my head.

When my mother left, for the longest time, I had felt nothing: white noise had filled the hole where my heart was supposed to be, everything around me was like static noise, and that had remained like this until Filípa.

The pain I felt was too much that I didn't even know it was possible. I hated her, and I loved her at the same time. I wanted to murder her and kiss her. I wanted to forget that she had ever existed, except that I didn't because the only thing worse than the crack in my chest would have been the numbness of before. Blindly, I fell for her, and she was there, solid, warm, and real. I buried my face in her stomach, and I sobbed; she laced her fingers with my hair and ran them through it, through my neck, my face. Soon she was kneeling in front of me, my face between her palms. Before I knew it, we were making love as we had never made it before: softly, taking our time to make sure that every kiss and every touch was just in the right place, breathing each other in deeply, but also carefully, rediscovering every crevasse, feeling, genuinely feeling each other's skin.

To hell with everything. She was with me now.

That was all that mattered.

Filipa

Sam held her, and she felt relieved that he was with her, that she wasn't alone. She tried to convey with her hands, with her skin, how much she loved him, how sorry she was that she had hurt him, how much she despised herself for being weak. Her face was still wet with tears by the time they had finished.

She could only hope now that he would see that she… what? Why had she ignored the voice inside that had told her to say no? This was nothing but the same thing that always happened to her. There was someone else inside of her, someone who wanted to see her fail, to punish and torture her, to sabotage anything she could hold dear. Filipa sat and hugged her knees. Sam was awake, staring at the wall, not at her.

"Sam," she whispered

"I can't do this," he whispered back.

She swallowed the knot in her throat.

"What do you mean?"

"All I see is him all over you."

Filipa looked down at herself, at her naked body. Why couldn't she help but feeling dirty?

They stayed quiet.

16

The interview

Samuel

Q.

I never thought I would want any of this.

Q.

A husband, a family. It's such a huge responsibility.

Q.

Being someone's mother.

Q.

It's so easy for women to erase themselves.

She looks down at her hands, pensive. I ask another question.

Q.

No, with Samuel, it was different. We found each other like only two people who are not looking for one another can.

Q.

I didn't feel the need to be the cool girl, the fun girl, or the smart girl. I could cry, but he wasn't the kind of guy that gets off on depressed girls.

She cocks her head and furrows her brow

I don't know. For someone like me, someone who has spent her entire life proving that she is not afraid of men, it was easy not to be afraid with Sam.

Q.

These are weird times to be pregnant, are they not? Every other day it seems like the world is gonna collapse. And suddenly, it becomes evident that everyone should be able to live in dignity and peace, even if they are unable to work. I was telling Sam the other day that it's so easy to throw around a phrase like 'the world is ending'. When the real hard times come for us, we'll regret saying things like those. It takes a long time for an empire to collapse, but I'm already starting to mourn it.

Q.

I've always been an indoors kind of person, ever since I was little. I could not understand why anyone would go out to play in the park when there was a nice cozy couch, a cup of hot cocoa and a TV inside. I hated it when the neighbor kids rang my doorbell and asked if I could come out to play; most of the time, I was just counting the minutes so that I could go back to my house, to my games, to my toys.

Q.

I liked playing alone. I made up my own games, my own stories which usually involved princesses (played by me) getting poisoned and falling into some charming sleep. Oddly enough, I don't remember a prince charming saving me. In my games, I liked sitting languidly on an imaginary chaise lounge, with a corseted silk and velvet dress on, my long curls whirling down my shoulder and past my waist, a delicate silver circlet placed daintily on my head. Not the most exciting of games, I guess, but I had a blast. I was the beautiful princess in the tower, and I spent my days singing out the window, tending to my gorgeous hair, smiling sweetly, reading books, writing, and dancing alone.

Q.

I still like playing alone, yeah.

Q.

I think I was trying to make my dream of being a princess come true. Without realizing it, I was trying to make myself the princess in the tower, like this one time that I accepted an invitation from a guy I met online to travel to another city and meet him. He bought me a first-class train ticket, an Audi picked me up at the station, took me to a fancy hotel where I checked in, and went up to a big suit. He came up about an hour later after I had taken a shower and had a glass of Dom, but the whole thing was new to me: I had only a vague idea of what this dynamic was, and I wasn't sure how to behave. I remember I hadn't even waxed; I had my long, curly pussy hair intact. We talked a little on the couch. He asked me what I liked, and I told him. He gave me instructions. I pretty much let him take the lead. I also remember telling him it was the first time I did anything of the sort. Somehow, it felt important. We didn't have sex. I blew him, and he slapped my ass until it was red, and then he got a call, left, and I stayed in the room and ate dinner until it was time for the car to take me back to the station. It only occurred to me later that he had made up an excuse to leave because I wasn't as hot as he was expecting, but the thought didn't bother me because, all in all, the experience had been quite nice. Accepting expensive things from a man I barely knew had been awkward though. The experience taught me one thing, and it was that, despite all the hours I had spent fantasizing about being an expensive escort, I didn't think I was up to the performance. It felt too weird to place myself in a position where my body was so blatantly interchanged for goods. I've never been one for dating rich guys. It turns out I'm not one for being bought by them either.

Q.

Sam's dad didn't leave him much. The house is more than enough. His mom lives in Sao Paulo. We are planning on visiting her as soon as we can. She looks a lot like him. We talked on Skype.

Q

The house is big, so there are a lot of chores, but we have a system in place now. Friday is bathroom day, so Sam takes the one upstairs, and I take the two downstairs. The second bathroom under the stair is tiny, and I take it because I'm faster. On Saturday, we do all the laundry. On Sunday, we vacuum the whole house, pass a microfiber rag over all the surfaces, wash the floor in the kitchen, and wax the hardwood floors. I like housework. I was always terrified of becoming a housewife, and now the thought is almost appealing. I don't know. I like making my own money though. I don't think that is something to be given up easily.

Q.

No, I still paint. We're getting by. I'm lucky I managed to find a job that pays well and leaves me time off. I don't want to be famous. I don't care about "making it." Our house is filled with my paintings. Sam loves them. He frames them, and we give them to our friends as presents. He keeps all of my sketches, even the nasty ones that I want to throw away. He also repurposed the upstairs room back into an art studio, and we have the crib there as well because we're painting it together. We don't know if we're having a girl or a boy, so everything is green, which is a color that I used to hate, but lately I like it.

Q.

I want to work. It's good to have a steady source of income, and the best part about Berkensdorf, about this northern town, is that I get to work a part-time job that still allows me to live decently without worrying about saving every penny for my baby's school, or college. I think about that a lot.

Q.

Sam reminded me of what is really good in life. Without him, I don't think I would have been able to look twenty years into the future, and now here I am painting my baby's crib, feeling good about the whole thing, forgetting about the shrinking Amazon, and the pending wars, the lab-made viruses, the wildfires in Australia, and the big strong men in the USA, Russia, and Iran playing with our fates as if we were objects. Sam may say that I reminded him what love was, but he reminded me of who I was. By loving me, he reminded me how to love myself.

He won me with that.

17

Atonement

Filípa

Wouldn't it be nice if that had been how it all ended? A house, a family, and a baby. A perfect life. But, alas, the mistakes that we make come back to haunt us, and there is no escaping the shadows of the past.

Filipa liked to have these interviews with herself. She liked to imagine what it all would have been like if she had been able to be happy and to allow someone to have all of her without holding back. She took a step back and appraised the painting she had been working on. It was a strange piece, with lots of clashing colors and infantile shapes. She liked the overall effect, she decided. The round faces and the big eyes were still there, but she had shifted onto more geometrical patterns, flatter imagery. She had left the ink behind to work with bright paint, acrylic over a canvas. This was the fourth painting in the series she was working on. There would be an exhibition in six months, a lapse of time that seemed incredibly long and way too short at the same time. The grant covered everything, and all she had to do was paint, which she had taken on to do with an almost zealous approach, pouring her every ounce of energy into the canvases, marveling as the figures came out. She relished this new approach where the emphasis was on feeling rather than technique, as she imprinted her most innermost self into the painting as if it was not only that extra something that made it come to life but an actual physical element that a potential spectator could see.

She hadn't seen or heard from Sam since she had left his house that November afternoon. The time in his house seemed like a dream, a blurry, cozy reality, an improbable ripple in the ocean of time.

"I can't do this," his words still hurt, and she liked to torture herself with the fake interview game.

What haunted her was not the possibility of what might have been, which had seemed improbable even at its most real, but the thought of having hurt someone who had loved her, embraced her, adored her. Filipa wasn't sorry that she had taken away her own dream, the thing that might have made her happy. Truth be told, it wasn't until much later, when she was alone at the bus stop wondering if she had enough money to pay for a hotel, or if she would have to call one of her acquaintances (Filipa didn't really have friends) in the hopes that they would take pity on her; that she realized what she had just lost: a chance at being Happy, with a capital H. The realization had hit her like ice. She hadn't really thought about that alternative. She had not counted on Sam seeing her with Wallace. She was going to tell him, of course, but he was already so angry that there was no going back. What a catastrophic coincidence that he decided to go just to that bar, just at that moment! She couldn't help but believe in God in moments like this, but not in the sweet forgiving God they had taught her about in school, which she doubted even existed, but the mean, vengeful God of the Old Testament, the one that seemed violent, petty and angry. He was so human that he might as well have been real.

Filipa wasn't sure if she believed in divinity or not, but it certainly did seem like something other than flesh and bone was at stake in the world, something ineffable, transparent, ungraspable, and it was that something that she tried to embed into her art, her paintings, which now laughed like someone who has stared into the abyss and had the abyss stare back: nothing to lose, nothing to gain, everything to be.

After leaving Samuel, after shutting tightly the door to a life with him, Filipa had found herself still alive, still on her own two feet, still watching the world go on around her. Nothing had stopped. Nothing had ended, except for her own little private world with Sam, their island for two in the middle of the whirlwind. That had ended, but it had changed nothing. In the end, the world was still there. Perhaps she had changed. She HAD changed. But it was too subtle of a change to be able to put it into anything other than abstract shapes and clashing colors.

There was another part of her that reminded her that it was also perhaps that elusive divine entity that some called God that had put the grant in her way. It all seemed so impossible before, all those voices that sounded so legitimate, so knowable, telling her that if she ever committed to art, she would starve or teach (for some reason those seemed equally bad), all those grownups, those people either laughing at her or looking at her with commiseration when she said that she wanted to be an artist when she grew up. Like Dalí, she would say as a little girl. He was her favorite growing up. The way the legs of the elephants went up, up, fragile like a spider's… Gala's face made up of bubbles.

And yet here she was, and it was all happening. She was 27, alone, and somehow still standing, doing what she had always wanted to do, and being ok. That was the thing. She had always seen herself as some kind of puppy in dire need of protection, she had always sought to exist under somebody else's umbrella, but when the opportunity had come to seize the moment, and start a life with someone, she had thrown it all away. She sighed and stepped back, wiped her hands, and turned her back to the canvas. Nothing else was gonna get done today.

It was okay, perhaps, to be one of those weirdos who don't do things the way they are supposed to be done. It was good to feel whole, and alone, with nobody to justify her but herself.

It was strange. She felt now like she had felt during those first months at Sam's house, during the lockdown, when there was no choice but to exist because the world had stopped going round. There had been breathing, eating, lovemaking, and she had felt whole, at peace, like she was finally, for once, the center point of her own universe, instead of being scattered all over.

Now the world had started turning again, and once more, she felt at peace. The vaccine had come and with it, the world had re-opened. She was fine. She was okay. Her little world had ended, but she had not.

Filipa had always been afraid of everything. Her entire existence had been an exercise on doing things she was afraid of. Choosing, and jumping, but always with that iron hand gripping her stomach, yelling at her to stop. With Sam, for the first time maybe ever, she had felt the grip loosen a little. She had stopped feeling torn, and it had been as if the whirlwind inside her had stopped, and she could finally breathe easy, look around inside herself and appreciate the view. Perhaps, however, what had happened had been akin to being in the eye of the hurricane. Things had been calm, but it had only been a false calm, and then the storm had returned in full force.

The Academy had re-opened after people started getting vaccinated, and she had returned with a new attitude. Wallace looked at her with new eyes. Almost like she was a completely different person. On some level, she was. Perhaps, she was only now finally coming into being the person that she had always been. A Filipa who wasn't constantly on the verge of panic. A Filipa that knew she could make mistakes, not be forgiven, and survive. A Filipa that now saw that hurting someone, having someone hate you, saying no is not the worst thing a person can do. The worst thing a person can do is lie to themselves.

Out of all people, it had been Wallace himself who told her about the grant. Perhaps he was trying to atone, but she didn't care. She had applied, worked harder than she ever had, and presented a proposal for a collection of paintings: *The Summer of borrowed time.*

Filipa had two new golden rules, and she had tattooed them on her left forearm: The first one was: Don't lie. The second was, "I always have two minutes to brush my teeth". One to remind herself that she didn't have to pretend to be different to fit in. The second, to remind herself that there was always a better way to use time than to watch an endless stream of YouTube videos. She was getting better at existing by herself.

If you make a home in somebody else's heart, don't be surprised to find yourself homeless.

She had been so eager to have it all done with, to be sure of one thing, at least one thing.

She had thought that thing could be Sam, and then she had ruined it all by herself by going back to someone who saw her as nothing but a prop. It had not been until after she lost him that she realized just how much she had grown to love Sam. The way his lips curled upwards when he saw her face, the incredibly sweet manner in which he held her face when he kissed her, the way he had made her feel at home from the second she had walked inside, the way he had let her talk about things that were difficult without interrupting, teasing her, or laughing, the way he seemed to understand her deeply without need for words, and the way he respected her silence, and just held her.

She had been so eager to hold on to something real that she had lost it. She had taken it away from herself.

On her desk rested the invitations for the show. Four. One was for Sam, she decided. He could burn it if he wanted, but it was still his.

Sam

"So? Are you going?" asked Jonah while he opened a bottle of beer and handed me another.

"I don't know. No. Maybe."

"Do you want to see her?" He took a loud sip from the bottle, I opened mine.

"Yes. No. I don't fucking know."

He took another sip of his beer. We were on our lunch break. After Filipa left, I had begun to spiral even faster than usual, but my anger was even stronger, and I decided I wouldn't let her beat me. My hurt, as per usual, became my fuel.

"You need closure, man."

"No, what I need is to never attempt to be in a relationship again."

"C'mon, man, don't say that. So, you got burned, so what? It happens to everyone."

I didn't reply and took a sip of my beer instead. I had never understood that point of view: everyone is miserable, so you have no right to be. Such a weird world we live in. Individualistic to a T unless it's actually time to advocate for yourself, then you are just a selfish ass wipe.

The really great thing about being a programmer was that I could get a job pretty much any time I wanted, and this one was suiting me just fine. It was a small company, there were only five of us and the hours were flexible, as long as we got the job done the bosses didn't really gave a crap if we took two-hour lunches or drank on the job.

"I think I might go."

The truth was, I wanted to see her even if just to tell her to her face, one more time, what an awful person she was.

"You should. Sounds fun. Plus, Rothenberg is nice. If you get there and don't feel like going to the expo you can just sightsee, or, even better, hole up in a pub and drink beer and eat sausages until you pass out."

Despite myself, I laughed. That didn't sound half bad, actually.

"I suppose."

"Seriously. Ever since I met you, all you seem to talk about is this girl and how she screwed you over. How you gave her everything and she just went and slept with someone else."

"She said she stopped it before the actual sex—"

"Whatever. The point is, you miss her. Look, she made a mistake. It happens. You said that she didn't really talk that much about herself or her past. So? Maybe she was dealing with some shit. Maybe she just genuinely screwed up and only realized just how badly after. In hindsight, it was 2020, you know."

"I can't just take her back."

"Sorry to be blunt, but you don't even know if she wants you back. She seems to be doing okay."

"Why else would she invite me to the show?"

"Maybe *she* wants closure. Maybe she just wants to see you one last time, and remain friends. Your breakup was pretty ugly."

"Dude, she fucking slept with someone—"

"I know, I know," Jonah said holding up his palms to me. "I'm not saying what she did was right. I'm just saying, I've sure fucked up in the past and I'm grateful every day my wife stuck by me. Because life is hard, and things are messy, and at the end of the day sometimes not even we understand our own motivations."

I scoffed.

"That sounds like something she might have said."

"I'm just saying, man. People are people."

He shrugged, and we drank in silence. A light breeze came in through the window. I closed my eyes. People are just people, indeed, for all, that's good, bad, or somewhere in between.

18

The Gallery 2.0

Filípa

It was a beautiful night. Everything was perfect. Filípa had a new dress. It was black with bolero sleeves and a big red flower embroidered on the skirt, which flowed nicely as she walked. Her heels were chunky, comfortable to walk in, but sky-high, and her hair was long enough now that it curled a little at the edges. She felt pretty, and she loved it. People were here to see her, to see her paintings, a whole year of hard work finally coming to an end.

She was overcome by a sudden feeling of sadness when she remembered, once more, that Sam had not replied to her invitation. She had had this fantasy, this idea, that he would take a chance on her again, and come, and walk into the gallery and see the paintings and realize that they were about him, about them, and forgive her, and kiss her, and maybe then everything could go back to being the way it was. Filipa shook her head and hands to get rid of the feeling. She had lost Sam, but she had gained something else, something that he had helped her find. That constant feeling of doubt, that voice inside her tugging her towards the shadows, he had helped her destroy that. He had seen her for who she was before even she had had a chance to.

"You saw me when I was invisible."

It was a line from the Princess Diaries, one of the greatest movies ever made, Filipa was willing to fight anyone on that. It was all about who sticks with you when you feel like dirt, who helps you up when you can't unbend your back, and who you take with you once you start to fly. In the sequel, of course, they had ruined everything, and Anne Hathaway (Filipa couldn't for the life of her remember the name of the character), had ended up with the generic hot blue-eyed mean-turned-nice guy, effectively ruining everything that had made the first movie great. In the first one, Mia (that was the name!) had not stayed with the hottest one, or the richest one, or the most charming one.

She had gone for the sweet one.

At 27 years old, Filipa was more aware than ever of the fact that there were many things she didn't know. Her phone rang. Why did we still say 'rang' when it was more like 'sang' or even 'sounded'? She slided her index finger upwards on the screen and answered the call.

"Yes?"

"Yes, Filipa, it's Anneke."

"Oh, hi, I was just about to head out."

"Stay put, I'm sending a car to take you."

"That's not necessary."

"It's not a problem, they will be there in twenty minutes."

"Well, if it's not a problem."

"Not at all."

"Thank you."

It was summer again. The pandemic was over, and while new strands of the virus seemed to pop up every couple of weeks, the scientists were keeping up as well. Not that all was well in the world. Not by a long shot. Water wars were looming in the future as the United States dried up its rivers and lakes, independent journalism was taking its last breaths, and back home people were taking to the streets to protest a government that seemed to take everyone's interest into consideration except for theirs. She felt both guilty and grateful. Who cared that Samuel wasn't coming? Who gave a rat's ass if he didn't love her? So what? Yeah, okay, she had made a mistake, but you know what? Mistakes happen, they make us who we are, and then we move on. There is no reason to dwell in the past. Was it Dumbledore who said that, or was it Gandalf? Filipa couldn't remember. The point was, what was done, was done, and she did not intend to spend another second forgetting that she was pretty much the luckiest bitch on the planet, that she had made everything she had ever dreamed come true, that she was in freaking Germany, in an adorable little town, presenting her work in a private gallery for potential buyers, thanks to a grant that she had won because of her talent, her creativity, herself. She had made all of that happen, and she was going to enjoy it, dammit! Sam could hole up in his house and ignore the world, but she couldn't be bothered, not anymore.

I mean, what else could a girl do? She had sent e-mails, texts, she had called, she had painted him thirteen paintings and… well, true, he didn't know about the paintings. He didn't know that the whole show was for him.

I put on a performance… I put on a show

Filipa swayed to the music in her head. Performance, by the XX.

I do it all so… you won't see me hurting…

Oh, Sam…

When my heart, it breaks. I put on a performance… I put on a brave face.

The rest of the lyrics flooded her completely.

Even when I was hiding, you could always find me… now you've stopped looking for me, but I'm still playing hide-and-seek… I want you to notice. But you just don't see.

And then, the punchline.

This show is wasted on you… so I perform, for me.

Yes. It was time to go. The doorbell rang, as if on cue.

That's right, Filipa thought as she climbed into the back seat of the town car. Her hurt over Samuel had been her fuel. She had used that paint and created something beautiful and now, she could finally let him go. Finally, now that the future didn't seem as blurry, now that she had finally had herself on her side, now that she could finally stop fighting, and she felt whole.

Perhaps she had also used Sam the way she had used Wallace. Looking for something inside them that would fix her.

The car pulled up to the building. Flowers were in bloom, the trees were decorated with LED lights wrapped around their trunks, the crescent moon barely visible in the dying sunlight. Filipa closed her eyes and allowed herself to enjoy the moment. This was hers, only hers and nobody else's.

Samuel

Of course. It was just like me. I was vaccinated, surely all I had to do was to show my pass… but nope. The exhausted Easy Jet lady looked at me like she was ready to murder me slowly. I couldn't blame her, but I had to try one more time. I just had to.

"But I'm *vaccinated,"* I said for the third or fourth time. "I have the freaking green pass, for God's sake!"

She finally lost it.

"Sir, do you even understand how vaccines work? Just because you are vaccinated does not mean that you have zero risks of getting infected. An airplane is a closed environment. It would be irresponsible of our part to let you in without a negative covid test. That's final."

Even though she was making perfect sense, it was now I who wanted to kill her.

"Miss, there must be something you can do. It is of the utmost importance that I get on that flight."

"Everyone has something of the 'utmost importance' sir," she snapped. "Now, either you move, or I will call security. So, move. *Now.*"

I gave up, rage boiling in me so vigorously that I would have loved to kick every single chair in the stupid waiting room and punch every single one of the stupid, idiotic, cow-like people, in their dumb, pasty faces. Particularly the phlegmatic old man sitting in his stupid wheelchair shaking his stupid spotty head from side to side and pontificating to his middle age toupee wearing son about the selfishness of today's youth all while the vile bald man looked at me with a smug smile on his face, exactly the same expression of a five-year-old enjoying watching another five-year-old getting scolded by the teacher in school. God. Some people just never grow out of wanting to please those around them. That was one thing I always liked about Fil. She seemed to be so past giving a shit about what other people thought that she almost didn't even acknowledge their existence. A wave of sadness washed over me. What was I doing? Did I even have any dignity left? Why couldn't I let go of someone who had hurt me so badly?

"She is a selfish cunt, and you are a hangdog without self-respect," said half of me.

"She made a mistake, she has apologized a million times, and she wants to see you," said the other.

Sophie forgave me every time I cheated, and every time, I lost more and more respect for her.

Would it be the same with Filipa? If I forgave her, if we tried to be together again, would she respect me less? Would she cheat again?

"That's what you are going to find out," said the other part of me. "You want to know if it is possible. You need to. Even if just to be able to stop thinking about it."

It was too late to get the kind of test that I needed to board the plane. Obviously, they didn't accept the fast ones, which would have made things easier. Fuck.

I thought about calling Filipa and explaining that I really wanted to be there, but that the airline wasn't cooperating with my desire to show up at the show unannounced and surprise her, but it felt so anticlimactic. Perhaps it was my mother's fault for making me watch all those romcoms with her when I was little, but I had sort of gotten it into my head that the only way to re-start a story was a grand gesture, something unexpected, something that would take her breath away, sweep her off her feet, all that crap.

Or maybe this was all for the best. Another part of me suggested going back to the house, smoking a fatty, lying in bed, and binge-watching some Netflix show… I had the days off from work already, and it sounded so easy and cozy, and…

No.

The cloud of Novocain. That's what Fil used to call it. That numbness that takes all over you until time collapses in on itself. No. I was not going back to that.

I was going to *act.*

I texted Jonah.

"They won't let me on the plane. Want molecular, not rapid test. I fucked it up before I even did anything. Lol."

"Did u write Filipa?"

"No. She doesn't know I'm coming."

"Dude, whyyyyy"

"…"

"k, I got it. Look, there's a Flix bus going in two hours. You'll be late, but you'll make it."

"Did you not read about the test?"

"They don't ask you for that if you travel by land. You got your pass, right?"

"Yep. Idk, maybe this is all a colossal waste of time. What if she invited me just to be nice? Or because she felt bad. I should have RSVP'd. I didn't. What if they don't even let me in?"

"Then you'll text her."

"She never even looks at her phone. It used to drive me insane…"

"Dude. GO. Remember the plan? It will be FINE."

"I'll be too late. It's pointless."

"Look, I bought you the ticket."

The message with the attachment arrived swiftly. *Okay*, I thought. I had just enough time to get to the station.

"Thanks, man."

"No worries. And remember, whatever happens, you can always buy some cocaine and a hooker ✌□"

"□□"

Conversation over, decision, taken.

Too overwhelmed to even think about the subway, I walked up to the taxi line and climbed into the backseat of the first available one.

"Where to?" Said the balding driver.

"23 Fairfax Street."

"They wouldn't let you on the plane?"

"Nope."

"Which is it, no vax, antimask, or no test?"

"No test."

"Ah, good. Please wear your mask"

I immediately made for the mask, but the man started laughing.

"I'm just messing with you, man. We are all gonna die anyway, am I wrong?"

I smiled and nodded, hoping he would leave it at that. He seemed to get it because he drove the rest of the way in silence.

As the wheels turned and the city passed by, my mind started to drift into its own ocean. Why hadn't I told her I was coming? Why did I feel this tightness in my chest whenever I even thought about talking to her? I was afraid. I wanted to see her genuine, unfiltered reaction when she saw me. Only that way would I know how she really felt. And then, maybe, I could understand how I felt.

Filipa

The curator had done an amazing job. The paintings told the story beautifully, and people were asking her questions, they talked to each other, discussing the colors, the figures, the titles. Perhaps it was the overwhelming relief of having survived a pandemic, but there was a feeling of newness in the air, of people eager to exist again as they once had: ignoring the world outside to focus on their own. Filipa wasn't sure if this was a good thing, but she went with it. She, too, was eager to forget.

"I have noticed the moon is present in almost all of your paintings," said a man with a heavy German accent and a mustache. "Does the moon have a particular meaning to you, as an artist?"

Filipa pondered this.

"Yes," she answered after about ten seconds. "The moon is such a presence in our lives. She controls the tides. She pulls us toward her, and she moves. Even when she is invisible, she is there. I feel like the strongest forces that move us are usually the ones we are mostly unaware of. What I want most is to understand myself. And the moon reminds me that, sometimes, all I have to do is let go. Stop thinking. I have no control over these forces. I can only walk with them, and discover where we go. At the end of the day, all I can do is be honest. To be honest, to me, is to look at things, and at people, as they are, at the moment, consciously removing the layers of 'the things I know,' the prejudice, and see them as something new. It's the Bene Gesserit concept of naïveté. Have you read Dune?"

"I saw the movie. I particularly like how Paul…"

They discussed film adaptations and their source material for a while, and Filipa got so wrapped up in the joy of the moment that she didn't even notice him, standing in front of a painting of the full moon looking down on the mountains around Berkensdorf, over a purple sky.

When she did, her heart started racing. It was as if someone had dialed down the volume in the room, from a 10 to a 3. He was standing there, hands in his pockets, smiling obliquely at the painting.

She approached him, heart thumping in her throat.

"Sam."

He turned around and smiled wider, one eyebrow slightly raised.

"Hey, Fil."

"You came."

"I did."

The biggest moments in our lives can also be the smallest. A gesture, a smile, a look.

Filipa had always believed in the God of small things. The one that watches over the ordinary, boring task of existing. Time stretches on in lapses of nothing and then when the defining moments come, you somehow manage to get out of your head for a moment and *feel*, take off the mask and undo the knot in your stomach. Lower the barriers. Filipa forced herself to relax, letting go of the tension she had been holding in her body.

"I saw this," he pointed at the painting. "The first draft of this. That morning, when I slept over at your apartment, for the first time. I was about to leave. But then I saw the sketchbook on the table, and while I was looking at it, you woke up. And I couldn't leave. I was too intrigued. I wanted to see."

Filipa smiled and bit her lip.

"And?"

"Yes?"

"Did you like what you found?"

"It was… not what I expected."

"Well, what did you expect?"

"Well… I expected the sweet, beautiful, damaged girl. I think I didn't see through it all until the end. Until you showed me who you really were."

Filipa's whole body tensed, but he was smiling.

"In a good way, I guess. You certainly had me fooled."

"Sam, what do you—"

"No, no, no, don't get upset."

"I'm not *upset,"* she said, her voice dangerously low.

He turned his palms toward her again in a peace gesture.

"I'm not here to fight. Look, all I'm saying is that I have realized I have a type. I like sweet, damaged girls, who have no idea how attractive they are. I thought that's who you were. But that's not who you are, is it?"

Filipa said nothing, her eyes alert.

"You are a clever, clever woman. You play the part of the damsel in distress so well because you know men will fall for it when in reality you are just using them as stepping stones to get to where you want to go."

"Sam, where is this coming from?"

"He is here."

"Who?"

"Him."

Her eyes widened with understanding.

"Oh, no, Sam, he's not with me, he just knows the owner of the gallery, the art world is small—"

"I don't care, Filipa. You invited me, knowing full well that the man you cheated on me with was gonna be here? After what happened?"

"I didn't even know you were coming!" she raised her voice, and a couple of people turned their heads towards them.

Filipa gestured with her head and led him towards a smaller room with a small writing desk, upon which a black cat peacefully slept.

Filipa closed the door.

"Why did you come here, Sam? To get another apology? I tried to apologize to you for a long time, during the six months I was in Berkensdorf before I got the grant, I must have called you a million times, I sent e-mails, texts, fucking smoke signals, and you ignored me completely. Then you show up, unannounced, and make a scene immediately?"

He scoffed and pressed the bridge of his nose, between the eyes.

"Look, I'm sorry. But seeing you so happy and then seeing him just made me feel like I was in the wrong place. I just…" He took his index finger to his temple. "I couldn't stop thinking that you cheated on me. Like a siren in my head."

"Once. It happened once. And we didn't even have sex!"

"Once's enough."

He looked as if he regretted his words, but he remained silent.

She inhaled through her teeth.

"Sam, I know I hurt you. And I'm so sorry. I was stupid, and impulsive, and dissociative, but I can't keep apologizing forever," she gestured towards the door. "What we had was beautiful, wasn't it? I thought that maybe we could get it back, but I can see that it was foolish of me to think so."

She looked at him, and her heart was overwhelmed with tenderness.

"You are never going to forgive me. Not really."

Sam stayed quiet; his eyes fixated on her.

"Are you?"

Samuel

To be honest, I didn't know.

"I wasn't ready to forgive you back then, Filipa. When you called, when you texted, I couldn't reply to you because I knew that if I saw you, I would fall, I would have no choice but to tell you I forgave you because the truth is, I wanted you back," he stopped, swallowed. "I wanted you back from the moment you left. But, what would that say about me? About my self-worth? And moreover, how could I ever really know for sure that you were being honest? People don't cheat out of the blue. People cheat because they are unhappy, but it's not even that, it's all those times that you said 'I love you,' it's all those times that we talked about what we would name our future children, it's all those times I respected your silence and said nothing when you blatantly ignored a question or stopped speaking in the middle of a sentence. It's all those times I told you things that I…" I gasped for breath. "God, Filipa!" my fists tightened. "I really wish you wouldn't have slept with that guy. I really wish you hadn't, but you did, and I don't get why. Why did you do it? Were you thinking about him when you were with me? Were you just biding your time, waiting for the right moment to leave me? What was I to you?"

She was looking at me, arms around her chest, her big eyes fixated on me, unblinking, waiting for me to go on.

"I gave you everything." even I was taken by the bitterness in my voice. "I gave you everything, and you paid me back with nothing."

"Paid? Is this how you see relationships? As a transaction of affection?" she scoffed. "Love is not an object. When you give love, you give it freely, you don't give it and then keep a receipt!"

"Oh, you definitely know about giving love freely."

Now it was Filipa who tensed up.

"Enough. I can't do this. I'm sorry for everything, I—" she stopped to take a breath. "I guess I thought this would go differently when I invited you. This was… a mistake."

"Filipa, you can't dictate when somebody's ready to accept an apology! I knew that if I talked to you back then, I would just snap and—"

"As opposed to what you are doing now?" she snapped back.

I closed my eyes and breathed through my nose to temper my boiling anger.

"You are the one who cheated on me."

"I know!" for a second the slight undercurrent of noise from the other room died down. When it picked back up, she went on, in a loud, furious whisper.

"I know, and there has not been a day in the past year and a half that I haven't thought about it."

She stopped for a second and frowned.

"But I'm done punishing myself. I could blame the alcohol, I could say that the situation got away from me, I could try and explain… but I can't, and I think it would only make things worse. So, all I can do is say I'm truly sorry that I hurt you, and move on from this because the war that you are fighting right now is not against me. It's against yourself."

I would not let it go.

"Wait. Are you saying I did something wrong? What? Were you unhappy? Were you upset quarantining and living rent-free in a five-bedroom house instead of a crummy apartment in the center? Tell me, what is it exactly that I did wrong?"

She looked horrified.

"Nothing! You did nothing wrong. You are a fucking martyr."

Her face was twisted into an expression that I had never seen on her face before: active, burning disgust.

"I'm leaving," I said.

"Good. Wait here 30 seconds after I go out, and then get out yourself."

"Fine," I said through gritted teeth.

"You know, Sam?" She said, head slightly turned towards me, hand on the doorknob. "I'm glad I painted this for you. I'm happy I painted our story. That way, I can remember you how you were then, and not how you are now." She moved to open the door, hesitated, closed it, and turned her head again. "For what it's worth, I really did love you. A lot."

With that being said, she threw back her shoulders and walked out the door.

I stood there; my fingers numb. I didn't feel angry, I didn't feel anything, except for a slight sense of bemusement. I had been unwilling to admit it, but I had been expecting *Sleepless in Seattle* and, I got *500 days of Summer* instead.

Of all things, I had to think about romantic comedies. Of course. I laughed at the absurdity of it all. Here I was, standing in a tiny room, waiting for a girl to come back and tell me that she loved me. I was Julia Roberts.

Thirty seconds had passed by now. I opened the door. The crowd had thinned somewhat, nobody gave me a second look, and she was nowhere to be seen. I walked by the paintings, and almost unwillingly slowed down. They begged me to look at them again, I had been so angry before, I had barely glanced.

I'm glad I painted our story, she had said, and it was true, it was all there. The house, the records, the coffee, the cat. The summer of borrowed time. I forgot about my decision to leave, and I went through the paintings again, one by one. The moon and the bus stop of the night we met, the ottoman in the living room, the kitchen with the window in the ceiling, my blue-gray bedroom. My father's studio, the kiss. As I saw our time together through her eyes, a warm feeling started to envelop me, from the core of my torso, between my ribs, all the way to the tips of my fingers. I laughed out loud. A woman to my right gave me a funny look.

I felt the hairs on my nape tingle. It was about time I left.

I didn't know how to feel. I'd never been very good at judging how I feel. It was something that I had hidden inside a box, long ago, and the key was somewhere inside a drawer with a million things inside. I had gotten very good at living rationally, at letting my intellect guide me without taking into account the part of me that didn't make sense, the part of me that insisted on going against what I knew was best. The part of me that felt.

With Filipa, I never had to explain anything. She seemed to understand how I felt, when to talk to me, when to leave me alone, when to be sweet, or when to be serious. I had never realized what an amazing ability that was. She was able to sense the mood and adjust accordingly. When we talked, she listened, asked the right questions at the right moment, helped me make sense of the noise inside. It had been invisible to me, that ability of hers, until I had found myself without it, sober and alone in a foreign city. As she had given it, she had taken it away. And now, I was afraid to look inside.

The realization struck me like lightning, and I stopped in the middle of the street. I was brought back by the blaring lights of a Volkswagen turning around the corner.

Safely on the other side, I took out my phone and googled someplace where I could sit down and maybe get some alcohol and food.

Heading southeast towards a pub that was rated 5 stars and had comments like *"Best beer I had in my life, great food, excellent service, all in all, highly recommended",* I started thinking that perhaps, that's what I had been doing my whole life. Using the women in it as feeling proxies, that is. It was all starting to make sense. When I was a kid, I could feel it in the air when my parents were anxious. My mother's mood depended on my father's, and mine depended on hers. If she was happy, I was happy. If she was sad, I was sad. When she left, there was no proxy. My father was a wall of silence, and I didn't know what it was like to feel on my own. How I was supposed to react to this. By constant anger? Confusion? Rebellion? All the above.

It was the summer of 2022. People still wore their masks outside; new vaccines were being developed rapidly to combat the new variants of the virus. It was safe to say that, even then, we still didn't see what was coming. We thought we had lived through the worst.

With Sophie, I had made her as wounded and miserable as I felt. When she had reacted with love and compassion to what I knew were unforgivable offenses, it made me hate her even more.

With Filipa, I had created a partner who needed nothing and accepted everything, someone who fitted me perfectly and in no way wanted me to change because she was easy-going and flexible, I had assumed that was all there was to her, that there were no edges, but I was seeing only part of the picture there. It was clear to me now, perhaps, it would have been worth it to dig a little deeper into her silence. Never like now did I understand that what is not said is just as, if not more important, than what is.

The city was wide awake, people still relishing in togetherness after their taste of isolation. It was strange. For me, 2020 had been a bubble, a chance at trying out a new method of living because the old one had been suffocating me. I had been living in isolation for years, purposefully putting distance between myself and the people who loved me, working hard to push them to the edges, so when they finally left I could blame them for not trying hard enough, not understanding, not forcing me to let down the guards but leaving me alone to fight my demons instead.

Filipa had disarmed the guards, easily. *It was real*, said a voice inside my head, and I immediately thought about the last hobbit movie and I started to laugh.

Tauriel

(In tears, holding Kili' s dead body)

Why does it hurt so much?

Thranduil

Because it was real

(Cue music)

The scene played out in my head. Why couldn't I stop thinking about cheesy movies? I sighed and went inside the first place I spotted with an open sign.

The place was alright. There was food, beer, and quite unexpectedly, free Wi-Fi. Next to the sticker with the network name and password, there was a QR code. It took me to a page where you could order directly without any human interaction. The post-pandemic brave new world was really shaping up to be an introvert's paradise.

The numbness was starting to recede somewhat, and I felt empty, a shallow shell, an idiot in the wrong place, at the wrong time.

19

Atonement II

Samuel

It was the time of scarves and hats, hot beverages, and yellow leaves.

"I was surprised you called."

"I was surprised you answered."

The air was toasty inside the café. Her hair was shorter, barely brushing her shoulders.

She brushed a honey blond lock back with her fingers.

"You seem well."

"Thank you. You look amazing. Really."

She was wearing a beige turtleneck and a double-breasted charcoal gray coat with open lapels. Her nails were done, and she exuded an air of casual elegance and wealth.

It had been almost three years since we had last seen each other, and we hadn't ended things in the best of terms. When I had called her, I had fully been expecting her to tell me to fuck of, but Soph had always been kind, and she had agreed to meet me. The café was fairly full, yet it provided intimate spaces, dark corners with low tables where one could have private conversations surrounded by the comfortable cacophony of public, anonymous lives, just a few steps away.

"Are you still working in that place?"

"No, they went bankrupt. I got a job a few months ago as a production coordinator for an advertising company. Nice people, good pay."

"A production coordinator? What do you do?"

She laughed.

"Well, you know… pre-production, mostly, making sure everything is ready to go for all projects, photoshoots, coordinating schedules, making sure everyone is ready… that kind of thing. It's pretty exhausting, actually, but I love it. It's a lot of responsibility, but I've always been good at performing under pressure."

Something inside me stirred when she said that.

"Yeah… too good, maybe."

"What do you mean?"

"Nothing, nothing. I mean, not about your job. That sounds amazing. Sounds like you are doing amazing. So, what else is up? What's been going on with you?"

"Well… I'm engaged."

Only then I noticed the sparkling diamond on her finger. She laughed.

"I thought that's why you called. Like maybe, you had seen it on Facebook or something."

I was stunned for a second, and then I reacted.

"Oh, shit! I mean, wow! Congratulations! I didn't know, I should have brought you a gift or something. That's a thing, right, engagement gifts?"

"I guess so," she said laughing. "So, you didn't know at all?"

"Not at all. I don't go on Facebook anymore. It's too full of people getting old. When did you get engaged?"

"Yesterday."

"Really?"

"Yeah."

"It would have been such an asshole move for me to do that on purpose, don't you think?"

We were both laughing.

"Oh my god, such an asshole move! All my friends told me not to come, actually. They said you were a narcissist and that the timing was really suspicious."

"I probably would have thought the same."

We laughed again. I sighed, wiping tears from my eyes.

"So… if that's not it, then why did you call? It's been a long time."

"I…" I inhaled sharply and plunged. "Lately I've been thinking a lot about us, about everything that happened, and… I… I wanted to say I'm sorry. I'm sorry I was so shitty to you. I'm sorry I made you feel like you were crazy when you told me you didn't trust me. You… you were good to me. You were doing your best and I just… I hated you for loving me… for forgiving me when I fucked up. I guess it made me feel even worse somehow… more guilty. Your kindness hurt. I took it all on you, all my anger, my frustration … and the whole time I thought I wasn't doing anything wrong because I never hit you. I wasn't hurting you, not really, you were just weak and stupid for staying with a bastard like me. It was your fault, for being weak. For putting up with it when you could just leave."

Sophie was looking at me, her eyes wide with surprise.

"Wow, I… wasn't expecting that. I… wow. That's… a lot." She took a sip of water and shifted in her chair. "So," she went on. "What happened Sammy? Who mistreated you? Who put you against the ropes?"

I smiled.

"Is it that obvious?"

"Well… I know you rather well."

At some point, the café had emptied almost completely. A very young waitress with a short brown ponytail was wiping tables across the room. Soft jazz played at a low volume. Sophie looked at me with narrow eyes.

"So? Who is she?"

"Her name is Filípa."

"Is she the reason why you are apologizing to me now?"

She looked at me, expectantly.

"I think so, yes" I replied after a couple of seconds.

"What did she do to you to bring about such an epiphany?" She asked with a smirk on her face.

"She did what I always did, I guess. She chose herself at the expense of others."

"Sounds like you have some resentment yet," she said crossing her arms across her chest.

"No, no." I laughed. "I'm done resenting people. It's a good way to get stuck in the past."

She uncrossed her arms.

I kept talking.

"She somehow managed to make me realize what you always tried to tell me." She leaned in over the table. "When we were together, Soph, I was angry, and I couldn't understand why you weren't angry too. I thought you were dumb for enjoying life and having a positive outlook when the world was so clearly crumbling into pieces. I guess, in my own tortured way, I was trying to teach you something. I saw myself as the wary grown-up showing the wide-eyed kid the ways of the weary world." I scoffed. "I don't know. The older I get, the more I think life is just about looking back and realizing what a total dumbass you were, and maybe get a little better. Decade by decade."

Sophie sighed, frowned, and leaned back into her chair.

"I didn't really know then, you know?" she said in a dreamy voice. "I didn't realize. I thought that's what girlfriends did. I was 22, and that's what I thought it meant to be a good woman. To ride or die."

"What do you think now?"

"That it's okay to get off the ride if it's killing you to be in it."

"Or if it's not fun anymore."

"All work and no play make Jack a dull boy."

"I don't know Soph… It's a brave thing, choosing to be happy. It's easy to dwell in misery, to get addicted to sadness. There's sweet pleasure in torturing yourself… a relief… when you are hurting inside, you either turn inward, and torture yourself, or you turn outward and torture others, but the pain always finds a way to deal with itself. That's why I'm not mad at her. She made me realize that."

She cocked her head.

"Pain demands to be felt."

"The fault in our stars."

"You hated that movie when I showed it to you."

"Nah, I liked it. I liked all the movies you showed me. I just couldn't admit it."

"Because they are for girls?"

"I hate to admit it, but yeah, probably."

"Pain will be felt, one way or another, so you might as well become aware of it."

Filipa had said something similar to me once.

"Some people walk around with a hole inside, so big, so dark, that it has swallowed them whole, from the inside out. They can't tell, you see, where the hole ends, and where they begin. They think they are the darkness."

"I was hurting too, back then. I don't know what this girl did to you, but the point is, she's not a monster. And neither were you."

She had reached across the table to take my hand, her eyes fixated on mine.

"It was, passionate, messy, miserable, and fun. It was all those things. It was not only bad."

There was a knot in my throat, I could feel tears running down my cheeks.

"Sam, you are not a terrible person. We are not defined by our mistakes. We are who we are because of them. Hopefully, we become more aware, we become better."

My voice came out quiet, shaky.

"I couldn't forgive her. I couldn't forgive her for doing to me the same thing I did to you more than once. But you forgave me every time." I sniffed and laughed. "How much of a hypocrite am I? What kind of person does that?" I laughed again, almost maniacally. "I am the embodiment of everything I've always pretended to hate. The phony who can dish it out but can't take it. What a fucking joke!"

"Is this the part where I'm supposed to tell you that you aren't a joke? I'm not your girlfriend anymore Sammy. I'm not gonna comfort you."

She sighed.

"You know, Sam, back when we were together, every time you talked down to me, or lied to me, or went with someone else,

I just assumed it was my fault somehow. I just defaulted into thinking that it was me who was doing something wrong, that I was somehow failing at making you happy."

"Soph—"

She put up her hand.

"The meaner you were to me the more I doubted myself, the more I assumed you were right, and I was wrong. That state of constant doubt was my new normal. Whether you loved me or not became my whole world, and when it was over, I thought I had failed in my mission. It took me a long time to understand that I wasn't responsible for your happiness."

She leaned back and put her hair up into a ponytail. I kept listening.

"You did what you had to do." Her tone was practical, as a matter of fact. "Stop finding reasons to punish yourself."

"What do you mean?"

She shrugged.

"Maybe you were just doing what you had to do. I mean, I, for one, think it's worse to falsely forgive someone than to not forgive them at all."

She had known. Filipa. She had seen. She knew before I did.

"So, you don't think I'm a two-faced bastard?"

"You are so hard on yourself. That's why you are so hard on other people."

The door of the café slammed, and we both looked up. An old man wearing a deerstalker hat walked in.

"I should get going," she said, getting up, gathering her things.

"It was good seeing you, Sophie."

"You too."

I got up, and we hugged for a full minute until she untangled.

"Bye, Sam."

"Bye, Soph."

I stayed there for a while longer, re-reading *The Catcher in the Rye* for the fiftieth time. It had been my favorite book for a long time. As a teenager, I had identified with Holden so much that it almost hurt to read. The boy who was too smart, too sensitive, too fucking honest for this phony world, this undeserving world.

I laughed quietly to myself.

I still liked the book, but I no longer saw Holden as the prophet for everything good and sincere. It was a strange feeling, looking back, thinking of myself as I read the book as a 15, 17, 25-year-old, and now, as a man of 35. Things change as you grow up. They get smaller. The stories that once made you tremble now make you laugh. The things that scare you now are much more ethereal and undefined than the monster under the bed.

I decided to go outside.

The moon was peeking over the mountains. A baby cried in the distance.

I smiled, feeling the promise of something new in the wind, the weight on my soul blowing away with the orange leaves rustling in the street. The streets too would blow away, eventually.

I was lucky, I realized with a new fire burning in the core of my body, that my life was truly in my hands. I could become the captain of my destiny, now that I was ready to get out of my own way.

"I hope you are well, Fil," I said looking up at the moon. "Wherever you are."

The lights in the street flickered, and the great silver eye in the sky smiled back.

The End

OTHER TITLES IN THE COLLECTION BY HAMPSTEAD HEATH BOOKS

The Dream Healer Saga (2022)

As long as he lives, he won't be able to go to the Afterlife; his consciousness will remain in the place we all visit during our sleep: Dream Realm, a surreal and ethereal reality **where everything we imagine materializes as soon as we think of it**, and **we move at the speed of our thoughts** but also a place ruled by mysterious spirits who feed on human fear **and grow it inside our minds and dreams, using our memory** and paradigms.

Join **Dream Healer** through the colorful streets of **imaginary cities and alternative realities**, in **an ethereal body** that is beyond the laws of physics and has the power to **create anything** that crosses his mind **as long as he doesn't spend all of his bodily energy**; join Ruth in her quest to break the boundaries of reality and discover the truth that concerns all of us; meet the clan of the Oneiromancers, those who control dreams.

Welcome to Dream Realm.

The Flock (2020)
A Cybernetic Horror Novel

Michelle has strived all her life to be perfect, both in her professional and personal life, and she actually is, that is until she wakes up one morning just to realize that she forgot everything about the previous day as though it had not happened at all; all she knows about it is that she suffers random panic attacks after seeing... a pigeon?

Why? What is the connection between pigeons and the day she erased from her memory? What is the connection between her memory and the ethereal digital space controlling everything in this world? Why does she remember a red-eyed hacker woman and a middle-aged man in a brown suit? What is the connection between her, the obscure cult known as "The Flock" and the strange figure they call "The Second Messiah"?

Are we protected from hackers just because we are organic?

Olivia (2019)
A Mystery Novel

Desmond Reed, university teacher, is a difficult person, that is true, he stole his best friend's girlfriend and married her just to drop her after she discovered she was infertile and became "kind of annoying," and then got one of his students pregnant in no time, but even someone like him doesn't deserve to get home and find his little daughter murdered in her own cradle.

This is how he ends up hiring his former best friend in order to find who committed such a horrible crime, but things are not always what they seem, and the investigations might end up revealing a soul-shaking secret from their past.

A criminal mystery that will have you at the edge of your seat as you wonder what everyone else is wondering:

Who is behind Olivia's death?

Realm.exe (2022)
Enter A New Reality

N. is a fairy tale princess. She lives in a castle, surrounded by servants, family members, and anything she could desire, except for one thing: memories. What is her real name? How did she get there?

Benjamin is an average twenty-year-old screw-up. No job, no family, no friends, and no money. Keiji is the son of evil billionaire CEO Keiko Takahisa; all he wants to do is to get back at her. Edgar and Evan are twins, separated from an early age and unaware of each other's existence...

What is waiting for them in the next step of human history, the upcoming solution for all of our world's problems and the final development of the next haven for us to find shelter?

LOG IN TO PARADISE! LOG IN TO REALM.EXE!

Valentina Ucrós-Acevedo was born in Bogotá Colombia on February the 5th, 1990. She is an Aquarius, Gemini rising. In 2016 she moved to Turin, Italy to study Storytelling at the Scuola Holden, from where she graduated in 2018. She currently lives in Italy, with her husband and Edgard, the black cat. **The Second Fastest Way to Happiness** is her debut novel.

www.ingramcontent.com/pod-product-compliance
Lightning Source LLC
LaVergne TN
LVHW091209150826
845672LV00005B/1296

* 9 7 8 9 5 8 4 9 6 3 0 1 7 *